This Book is Dedicated to

Barb,
who encouraged me
to complete this novel.

Other Books
by
Sandra Muzyka

How to Make Money Flowers
Finding Thorold
Waiting for Santa
Pesky Bees
Lily and Tad
The Art of Expression
My Dog's Life
My Cat's Life

CHAPTER 1

My story begins in a small town named Carleton Falls. A quaint little town where everyone pretty much knows everyone else. You just can't move around without someone knowing how far you've gone or how long you have left your house, and everyone knows where you're going.

Now, that can be a good thing or a not so good thing. Especially if that said person doesn't want others to know their business. You see where I'm going with this, don't ya.

Well, it was a beautiful warm September day when Maggie decided to go on a camping trip to the Carleton Falls State Park, where a small river flows through it. Soul River it was named, and largemouth bass could be caught there. It was the place to go when on vacation or if you just needed a few days' rest. It's just so peaceful and serene there. The trees will be turning their beautiful autumn colours and the river so crisp and clear; all of nature calling your name. I've been there, I know firsthand. There's just nothing like it.

Now Maggie, she is the daughter of my best friend, Sue. Sue could arm wrestle with the best of them. She was only 5'6", slim build and the curliest hair I ever did see. My mom used to tell her, "Take off that cap; you're smothering all those pretty curls." She would just laugh at my mom. Sue's eyes were big and a beautiful green in colour. She had the most captivating smile you ever did see. She has since moved away, which is another story, for another time.

Her daughter Maggie looks a lot like her mother, only slightly taller. Why either of these women would need a man around, is a mystery to me. There was nothing they couldn't do, and I have pretty much seen it all.

Like the time when Maggie got up on the roof of her house and took all of the shingles off with a shovel. A shovel, can you believe it? Then she turned around and shingled the roof herself. It took her a few days, but by George, she did it and a good job too.

I asked her if she needed any help and she told me 'No thanks,' sweet girl she is. She makes me Shepherd's pie once in a while, since she knows it's my favourite. My grandmother, who grew up in Scotland, used to call it Cottage pie. The only difference she said was the meat used; Cottage pie had beef and Shepherd's pie had lamb. Maggie calls it Shepherd's pie and uses ground beef. Either way it's mighty good. Sometimes Maggie would make me a cherry pie too. Oh my ... don't get me started on that cherry pie of hers ... mmm-mmm. I wish I had a piece right now. Well, anyway, she is a great gal. Ah, where was I? Oh yeah, there was nothing she couldn't do.

Every once in a while, she would take time off from her bakery business. Now you know why her pies are so good. Yep, she is a professional. Her business is called Magpie Bakery. A symbol of good luck and fortune, she told me. She has a brain for business too. Yes siree, smart girl.

At Christmas time she sells this Christmas plum pudding pie. Can you just imagine? Oh my, it's so delicious you can only eat one slice, truly, I kid you not. That's because people can't resist it and there's none left for seconds. My mother used to make plum pudding, but not a pie. Her pudding was so tasty, but with Maggie's pie you get the rich taste of plum pudding baked in a heavenly pie crust, so light and flakey. Well, there is just nothing like it and probably why people come from all over to buy some. I told her she needs to sell them country wide, but she just laughs, telling me it's nice to bring people to Carleton Falls, especially at Christmas time. We have a tree lighting event at the Carleton Falls Town Square, Christmas plays in the church auditorium and eggnog and hot chocolate parties throughout the town. The whole town is lit up like a fireworks display.

She would make cookies for all the kids and grownups to hang on the town square Christmas tree. That is if they weren't eaten before they got to the tree. But Maggie knew this and had boxes of cookies made ahead of time, just for this occasion. Once in a while she would let me help her at the bakery.

"Now make sure there is enough icing on the cookies," she said, "now add these sprinkles on top, Charlie."

Oh yeah, that's me, Charlie. On and on she would go, making sure each cookie was perfect. I can tell you from experience her cookies were so tasty. The aroma hit your nose first, then making your mouth drool for just one bite. The sweet sensation of that first bite was overwhelming and when you did there was no stopping. Your teeth would sink into a creamy yet fluffy center that was mouthwatering with a hint of cinnamon and a creamy buttercream icing that was to die for. The cookies that were made for the town square Christmas tree didn't have any icing or sprinkles on them. Maggie said that after Christmas the tree was taken to Carleton Falls State Park so that all nature could enjoy her cookies that were hanging on the tree. She even gave me a cookie to hang on the tree.

"Here's one for you too, Charlie," she would say. "Now don't forget to make a wish when you put it on the tree."

Always thinking of others. Now you see why Carleton Falls is such a great place to be. Just wait there's lots more. So where was I, oh yeah, Maggie on her trip to Carleton Falls State Park. I sat here as she packed her car.

"Hi Charlie," she called over. "Here you are, I made some banana bread for you. Don't eat it all in one day, either."

Well, she definitely knows me and baked goods.

"Come on, Jasper," she called, "get in the car."

Oh, did I tell you she has a dog? Yep, Jasper; great looking dog. It's an Alaskan malamute. They

CARLETON FALLS

A NOVEL BY
SANDRA MUZYKA

are great together, like peanut butter and jelly. Jasper is always around protecting Maggie and Maggie is always playing and taking care of Jasper. With the car filled with fishing and camping gear and Jasper in the passenger seat, Maggie was off.

"Bye Charlie, see you in a few days," Maggie yelled over. "Stay out of trouble," she laughed.

As if I could get into any trouble, funny girl.

"Okay, Jasper, off we go to the great outdoors, peace and quiet. With any luck we just might have fish for supper, boy. I'm glad the marina in town had some bait otherwise we would be making granola balls."

They were only a half-hour away by car. The sun was so warm and bright; its rays were hitting the hood of Maggie's car. She pulled down the visor and turned on the radio. Nothing too resonating, otherwise Jasper would start to howl. Fishing should be good, Maggie thought, as bass were pretty plentiful in the river. She had always caught a fish whenever she came. People would come from miles and miles to vacation at Carleton Falls State Park. There wasn't a time that the bed and breakfast in town didn't have guests. It didn't matter what season it was; tourism was always great in Carleton Falls. The traffic flow was good, and they arrived right on time, as Maggie pulled into the park. This was the best part of the drive, going from civilization to the wilderness and having a few park amenities didn't hurt either.

"Well, here we are, Jasper," said Maggie.

Jasper could smell the freshwater surroundings with a hint of pine in the air. Some of the trees had already turned beautiful shades of yellow and orange. The campsite she picked was the same one her and her dad used to stay at. Large trees and saplings surrounded the site with a fire pit in the middle. The land was level and off to one side were bushes and shrubs along with pines and cedars separating them from the other campsites. Throughout the years succulent new growth had emerged, making this site even more private. We'll have time to enjoy the view later, Maggie thought. It was important to put up the tent and get settled, just in case it rained, and then they would have shelter. Before coming, Maggie had checked the weather for the next few days; and no rain in sight, but she also knew the weatherman was not always right.

"Here boy, you can carry this bag."
Jasper was used to how things worked once they got to their destination. He would help carry the camping gear to the site. Then he would sit and watch Maggie put up the tent. Maggie laid out the base of the tent, ready to peg the corners into the ground.

"Almost done, Jasper, now for the middle pole and up she goes."

Jasper was barking and barking and going in circles, letting Maggie know she did a good job.

"I suppose we should go catch supper, Jasper."

Again, Jasper gave another bark in confirmation. Maggie actually thought Jasper knew what she was saying or maybe it was just the way she said it. Sometimes Jasper would go into the river and try to catch his own fish. One time he came out of the water with a great big crayfish attached to his nose. Jasper just thought it was playing and shook it right back into the water. When he looked for it again, he couldn't find it; the crayfish not liking the game Jasper was playing.

As they walked along the river's edge, Maggie was looking for her favourite spot to fish. With the underbrush being so overgrown it was hard to find it but she always remembered a formation of rocks surfacing above the water to give her a reference point. She could rent a canoe or rowboat, but Maggie liked to fish from the bank. This also gave Jasper time to go into the water as well, he just loved the water. She tried him in a canoe one year and it didn't end well. They both had a swim that day.

"Okay, Jasper, let's try here."

Maggie's dad taught her a lot of things and fishing was one of them. They used to go on a lot of camping trips together. Maggie's dad was the one who caught the biggest largemouth bass the town had seen. It had to be the grandfather of all fish. He took a picture of it, had it weighed and measured, then threw it back in.

He said, "If it had lived this long and evaded being caught, he deserved to live out the rest of his life."

Maggie thought her dad was the greatest. He would have been proud of Maggie and what she has accomplished in life. She was so much like him. Probably why she never married. No one could even come close to the man her dad was.

Maggie reeled in her line out of the water.

"Oh, almost got one, Jasper, but it took my worm."

As Maggie put another worm on the hook, she was watching Jasper trying to catch minnows along the bank, just another game to Jasper. The minnows were far too quick for him. It kept him busy and tired him out so Maggie could have a peaceful night back at camp. Ready to cast, she put her finger on the reel, threw her arm back and then forward, letting the line sail through the air as she lifted her finger off the reel.

"Oh no, where did he come from?" she said under her breath. "Sorry I didn't see you," she called. Yep, as luck would have it, the hook landed right on the man's sleeve.

"Are you sure you're out to catch fish?" said a deep rugged voice.

"I'm so sorry, I went to swing the line out and saw your canoe at the last second, but it was too late to stop the throw."

The man took the hook carefully from his sleeve and put it back into the water.

"Here you go, try catching a fish this time," the man called out, with a laugh.

So embarrassed, Maggie threw out her line again. She couldn't stop now because fish was going to be their supper. The canoe had gone passed them and was out of sight. Any fish caught today would be for their eyes only. The river was quiet now and the fish should be biting. Almost ready to call it quits for the day and a handful of worms later, there was a big splash in the water; Maggie's pole bending as she reeled it in.

"Look at it jump, Jasper, it's a big one!"

Maggie slowly reeled it in, giving the fish a little play on the line to tire it out. This way once it was close to shore; she would be able to bring the fish up onto the bank. Up and over and there it was.

"Look, Jasper, here's supper, finally."

It was a great looking largemouth bass, big enough to fill their stomachs. All Maggie had to do was fillet the fish and start a campfire.

"Come on, Jasper, let's get to camp and eat."

Off they went with a nice trophy in hand. Hopefully the bounty would be easier if not better tomorrow. But then again, that was the thrill of going camping and fishing. It brought her closer to her dad's memory. Minus the canoe incident, all in all it was a great first day.

Maggie got the campfire going and brought a cast iron pan to cook on. The cast iron pan held the heat and with a little bit of butter the fillets were put into the pan. She made sure to take off the scales while filleting the fish, just like her dad showed her. You could hear the skin sizzling in the butter, getting crispy. Everyone has their own way of cooking bass. Her dad loved to cook bass with the skin on. He said it protected the meat while cooking. Outdoors it was on the grill, indoors he liked to deep fry it, skin off. Four minutes later Maggie turned the fillets over, cooking them on the other side, all the while basting them in the butter. All that was needed now was a slice of fresh bread, which Maggie remembered to bring. Jasper was sitting patiently waiting as he knew the aroma of Maggie cooking fish from the last time they came. He knew the feast was coming any second. Out of the pan Maggie took the fish and plated them; one for her and one for Jasper, letting them cool before giving any to Jasper.

"Okay boy, here you go, enjoy."

It didn't take them long and their meal was finished. While cooking the fish, Maggie had also put on a pot of water for her instant coffee. With Jasper at her side, they both sat looking into the night sky. Sipping on her coffee she was so relaxed. This is what she had needed. The bakery was becoming busier than normal, plus she was thinking about putting an ad in an out-of-town paper. She realized that people would drive as long as an hour away to get what they want. If the business was to get a lot more customers, more than she could handle, she would have to hire more employees to help and maybe even expand her business. But tonight belonged to her and Jasper, as they watched the night sky, full of shooting stars. So many, you could almost touch them. What a beautiful site.

"Well, Jasper, time for bed."

Maggie added water to the campfire, making sure it was out. Then into the tent they both went; Maggie in her sleeping bag and Jasper curled beside her, just like home.

CHAPTER 2

Maggie opened her eyes to see a crack of sunlight coming through the screen-covered window, Jasper still snuggly lying beside her. A woodpecker tap-tap-tapping on a tree was her wake-up call. He was persistent and not giving up anytime soon, looking for insects within the bark of a tree.

"Well, boy, time to get up."

Neither Maggie nor Jasper wanted to get up. Maggie peeked at her watch pressing the button to illuminate it.

"Wow, ten to eleven. It's almost lunchtime, Jasper. Well, good thing I brought some kibble for you and granola bars for me."

Maggie now thinking she should have brought a few sandwiches as well, as the fishing might not be as promising as it was years ago.

"Come on, Jasper, lots to do before lunch."

Maggie unzipped the opening of the tent and out ran Jasper. While inside she got dressed and rolled up her sleeping bag. She needed to go down to the river and get a bucket of water to wash with. Also, with her hair being so curly and sleeping on it all night, she definitely had bed head. The curls were everywhere but where she wanted them. She knew she had to wet them down and arrange her hair again. She didn't want to use the water she brought. That was for coffee and Jasper.

Coffee was the most important commodity to Maggie. It's what got her day going and some throughout the day kept her on track, especially with the business being so busy.

Maggie even had some of her baked goods in other businesses in town. Like the Carleton Falls Mercantile and Katie's Bed and Breakfast. She made the best croissants. She even left some samples at the grocery store, a few miles away in Hainesley called the Stop 'n Shop. Maybe Charlie's advice would pay off. Anyway, nothing ventured, nothing gained, that's what her dad also told her. It doesn't hurt to try new things or expand on old things. Life can take you in all directions. It's which path you follow that matters.

Maggie made her way to the river's edge. Leaning over the bank she tossed the bucket in holding the handle tight. As she swung the bucket, her foot slipped off a rock. Then there came a big splash. Not only did the bucket go into the water, so did Maggie. Jasper, barking frantically, jumped in, trying to help Maggie.

"Well, that's one way to catch a fish."

There was that rugged voice from yesterday. Maggie didn't want to look up to see who it was.

"Here, give me your hand."

She lifted her head to lay eyes upon the rugged voice.

His hand, strong and warm, firmly grasped hers and gently pulled her up towards his chest. He was wearing wading pants and boots, definitely a Paul Bunyan type, tall, strong and very handsome. His dark brown hair was messy and a piece of it came over his brow teasing the wind to blow it backwards.

"There you go. Are you all right, Miss?"

"Yes, I'm fine, thank you," said Maggie, again so embarrassed trying to regain her composure.

"Is this what you were trying to fetch?" he said, as he leaned down to retrieve the bucket filled with water.

Maggie couldn't help noticing his arms and chest, his biceps protruding through his T-shirt as he lifted the heavy pail of water out of the river. Trying to hide the fact that she was looking, she played with her hair trying to comb it with her fingers.

"Yes, thank you," she blurted out.

"And who's this?" he asked.

"This is Jasper. Thank you again for your help, but we weren't in any danger. Jasper and I have been swimming in this river before."

"Oh yes, it looked like you had everything under control," he smiled. "You have yourselves a great day. If I can be of any additional help, please let me know. My campsite is down towards the river's edge."

Off he went, with Maggie literally fuming inside. How did he know where her campsite was? she wondered. Has he been spying on her this whole time?

"Who does he think he is, treating me like a little girl? We can take care of ourselves right, Jasper?"

Back to camp Maggie and Jasper went forgetting about the bucket of water. She could grab it later. Well, it wasn't Maggie's plan to have a swim, but at least her hair was drying nicely into the spiral curls she loved. Her hair was just wash-and-wear. With her life being so busy it was one less thing to deal with. Still upset at herself, she hung her clothes out to dry on a tree branch. The day being so warm it would take little time to dry her clothes. Another bonus she thought since she only brought one change of clothing.

"Come on, Jasper, plan B."

Off they went into the forest area that was well marked out. You couldn't get lost if you tried. There were benches to sit on as you passed by on the dirt path. Signs everywhere, even Jasper knew where they were going. Yep, a small store with just the essentials. Also, to the left of the store, a small boat ramp for canoes and rowboats. You could bring your own, but you could rent them too. It was a great little business run by her friend and her husband.

"Hi Kim, how are you?" Maggie asked.

"Hi Maggie, I'm great. Dale and I have had a good year. This year has been especially busy for us. More people are coming this way now and I think more people are traveling closer to home. Maybe they figure it's time to see what's in their own backyard."

"You're probably right, Kim, I have noticed a difference too with the bakery."

"What brings you and Jasper to the store? You usually bring everything you need with you?"

"I really came for a coffee, Kim. Jasper and I got up late and when I went to get water from the river, I slipped in."

"Oh my, are you all right?"

"Oh yes, an arrogant man came to my rescue. I was so annoyed and so embarrassed. It was the second time we had a run in. So much for a quiet retreat."

"Wow, that doesn't sound like a great beginning to your day. Well, here's a coffee Maggie, it's on me. Let this be the start of your day."

"Thanks Kim, you're the greatest. I'm going to need to buy some worms. I used quite a bit fishing yesterday."

"Yep, here your go, one box left. The bait guy comes tomorrow with fresh bait. It sure doesn't last long around here."

"Not with me fishing," laughed Maggie. "At least the fish are well fed. Thanks again Kim, nice to see you."

"You too, Maggie, take care!"

Maggie and Jasper walked back to the campsite. While drinking her coffee, Maggie took in her surroundings, feeling the warm breeze on her sun-kissed face. The sound of the birds in the trees made her think of her Christmas cookies. She had been pondering the idea of a new cookie, even though everyone loved her sugar cookies that were a combination of short bread and sugar cookies. It was a recipe that Maggie got from her grandmother,

Alice. Alice was such a wonderful cook and baker. Maggie would sit at the kitchen table rolling out the dough her grandmother gave her to use.

"Mags, now roll out the dough as even as you can honey," her grandmother would say. "The cookies will bake more evenly and take the same time to cook. We don't want any raw cookie dough."

How Maggie loved being around her grandmother. Alice was her mom's mother. Just like two peas in a pod. Maggie never knew her other grandmother as she had passed on when Maggie was a baby. Her mom's father was a quiet man and would agree to anything if it made you happy, very easy going, the complete opposite to her dad's dad, who was quite strict. Everything had to be a certain way. He was probably that way because he had been in the army. His ways had rubbed off on Maggie too. He taught her to be neat and tidy. Respect your elders and the people you meet, because you never know why they were sent your way. This got her thinking of the guy who helped her out of the water. After thinking about what her grandfather said about people sent your way, she decided to forget what happened and carry on with her day. The day was too beautiful to harbour any ill feelings and ruin the time her and Jasper had left.

Making it back to the campsite, Maggie grabbed her fishing pole, and a fold-up camp chair, not forgetting the worms she just bought. To the left of the campfire, she noticed her pail of water sitting there. He must have carried it up here she thought, which made her more furious.

"C'mon boy, let's go."

Maggie and Jasper headed to the riverbank. What a better way of calming the nerves.

"Let's try a little further down, Jasper," Maggie said.

Finding a spot, Maggie set up her chair. Next, she put a worm on the hook. Looking to make sure there were no boats or anything in her view, she pressed her finger on the reel, threw her arm back then forward as she let go of her finger on the reel. What a perfect cast she had made.

She sat down holding onto her rod waiting for a fish to hit her line. Jasper was patiently sitting beside her. The sun was high in the sky now, around two o'clock, she thought. There was really nothing to do but enjoy the view and relax, which is why she came in the first place.

"I just got a nibble, Jasper. This is a lucky fishing hole. I just know it. Wait and see, boy," Maggie said, trying to convince herself more than Jasper. "I got one!"

She stood up to reel the fish in, what a nice fish it was. Not as big as last night's, but still a good size.

"Look boy, supper."

Having taken the fish off the hook, Maggie secured it onto a snap chain stringer, slipping the fish's gill and mouth over the open latch and closing it. She placed it in the water being careful not to fall in and secured the other end on shore with a peg. This would keep the fish fresh until they went back to camp. Wanting to try for another fish Maggie added another worm to her hook. Again, she watched as her line sailed through the air and landed in the water. One more fish like this would make for a great supper for her and Jasper, she thought. Again, they both sat patiently waiting for a fish to bite. It was getting a little cloudy now with the sun peeking out only once in a while from behind the clouds. Still warm though, for a September day. The scenery was so picturesque. Maggie wished she had brought her camera or phone. She left her phone behind because she really didn't want to be bothered with calls from work. If it was an emergency, they could call the park store or even drive to get her, after all she wasn't that far away from town.

Maggie had closed her eyes for just a second, just relaxing and taking all the peacefulness in. Jasper had left her side to explore the flight of a butterfly. In and out of the bush it flew, then finally landing on Jasper's head. Just another one of Jasper's friends, Maggie thought. The last time they came Jasper helped a turtle get to the water. The poor thing was at the campsite not knowing which way to go to the river. Every time the turtle moved Jasper nudged it in the right direction. It kept Jasper busy all day and the turtle finally made it to the river.

Then there was Mr. Hampton's dog Daisy. It was a cute, small, white Maltese, a beautiful dog and Mr. Hampton's baby. They did everything together, just like Maggie and Jasper. One of the kids from another campsite left their inflatable raft-like floatie on the edge of the shore. Sure enough, Daisy decided to get on board and down the river she sailed. What a sight, Mr. Hampton was yelling in a frenzy about his little dog sailing down the river. Waving his hands in the air hoping someone would help him. Daisy didn't like to swim. The closest she got to water is when he took her to be groomed. Jasper heard Daisy barking and immediately ran to the river. In he dove and grabbed the floatie in his mouth and brought Daisy safely back to shore. It's a wonder Mr. Hampton didn't have a heart attack that day. He loved Daisy so much and couldn't thank Jasper enough for saving her. Now when Mr. Hampton sees Jasper, he gives him lots of treats. He is a very nice man, quiet and very pleasant to talk to, with a charming manner. He's retired now and could visit the park anytime but told Maggie his favourite months to come were June and August. He enjoys the park as much as Maggie does.

"Jasper look, another one, boy."

Maggie got up from her chair and reeled the fish onto shore.

"Another, good size, Jasper. Now we can head back and have our fish fry tonight."

CHAPTER 3

Maggie collected some firewood and got the fire going before cleaning the fish. She wanted to make sure the fire was hot enough by the time she was ready to cook.

While Maggie was cleaning the fish, Jasper had spotted a chipmunk under a log. Jasper was a very gentle dog and curious as to what the chipmunk was doing. In and out from under the log the little chipmunk ran playing hide and seek with Jasper. Maggie taught Jasper to be gentle around other animals. Mrs. Abigail, next door to Maggie had a cat and a bunny that Jasper loved to play with. He was so gentle they would come up to him and nuzzle his legs. So, this little chipmunk had no worries playing with Jasper.

Into the pan the butter went. Now the fish went in. The aroma from the fish was filling the night air. Maggie was also brewing some coffee in a percolator that fit on the grill. She wasn't having instant coffee tonight. Even the smell of brewed coffee was intoxicating.

While Jasper was still having fun with his newfound friend, Maggie had plated the fish, to cool off. Five minutes had passed, and she called Jasper to eat. He didn't have to be called twice. If Jasper could have anything other than kibble, he was all for it. What an end to a somewhat interesting day, to say the least. Maggie and Jasper sat and looked at the stars in the sky. The clouds had dispersed and nothing but clear skies. It was another fantastic night, and Maggie was looking forward to a freshly brewed cup of coffee. Maggie had learned how to make brewed coffee from her grandmother, Alice. It consisted of eggshells and salt. Both helped to make the coffee less bitter, plus a few other ingredients.

Jasper started barking, letting Maggie know there was someone or something coming through the bushes.

"Hello," someone yelled as the rustling of leaves got louder. "Good evening," said that same rugged voice. "I could smell the aroma of perked coffee from my campsite. It's not often a smell like that comes my way. I haven't smelled coffee like that in years."

"And I suppose you'd like a cup," said Maggie, a little reluctantly.

"Only if you have one to spare."

"Of course," said Maggie, trying to be courteous. "Here you are. I'm Maggie by the way, and you are?"

"Thank you, my name's Jack, nice to meet you, Maggie. How was the fishing tonight? Catch anything?"

"Yes, two nice-sized bass, which was lucky for us because I didn't bring any food except granola bars, kibble and fresh bread. So, it was good."

"Why's that, I mean, why not bring other food?"

"Well, I used to go camping with my dad, and we never brought food for lunch or supper. He taught me how to eat off the land. If we didn't catch fish, then there were berries or mushrooms and even greens for a salad. He has since passed. He knew my favourite food was granola bars. So that was the one thing we would bring. It was a breakfast food to get us going in the morning, plus granola was good for the birds too. He was an avid birdwatcher."

"Sorry about your father. He sounds like a very special man."

"Thanks, he was. He didn't have any boys to raise and couldn't see why a woman shouldn't know how to do man-things, like using tools, building things, fishing, filleting fish, shingling a roof. Anything he knew how to do, he taught me. I was fortunate that way."

"Yes, I see that. There are not too many women that would go camping by themselves either," said Jack.

"I guess you're right, I really never thought of it. I have Jasper and we take care of each other. Really, everything my dad taught me has made me outdoor confident. Just another place I belong, it's home to me."

As Maggie was talking, Jack became more intrigued. He noticed the fires reflection glowing in and out of every blonde curl on Maggie's head. Each curl framed her face perfectly and her complexion was radiant and luminous as a warm summer's day. A very earthy, down to basics, kind of girl he thought. A girl with substance, not one of those flighty can't do anything types.

"Thank you for bringing up the pail of water, Jack. I assume it was you. It was a little heavy, but I would have emptied some of it and retrieved it in the morning," Maggie stated, not wanting Jack to think she wasn't capable.

"Yes, I saw it still sitting there and thought you could use it. It was no problem. This coffee is a great ending to my day, quite delicious. Takes me back to my childhood when Grams would make some for Papa. I wasn't old enough to drink it but remember the smell throughout the house. Funny how the smell of something can take you right back to those days. Those were good times. She also made homemade bread. She would leave it to cool on the window ledge. On my way home from school, that's all I could smell in the air, Grams' bread. She must have seen me coming, because she had a couple of slices on a plate, still warm with butter and honey on the bread. As if the savory smell wasn't enough to get your taste buds going, it was that first bite, the anticipation of that first bite. The fluffy and airy dough was slightly heavy with hollows and crevices throughout. Then your taste buds would find the butter sunken into those crevices with the honey as backup, draping over the entire slice. It was truly heaven, and each bite was as good as the next. Only Grams could make bread like that."

Maggie saw the passion in Jack's eyes and the joy in his heart as he was talking about his grandmother. They had a great connection like her and her grandparents. She noticed his eyes were a hazel brown and every mention of his grandmother made his eyes gleam with endearment. It was so nice to hear wonderful childhood memories. For a brief moment, there was silence.

"Well, it's getting late Maggie, and I thank you for the amazing coffee. If you need anything, please don't hesitate to ask."

"Thanks, Jack, Jasper and I will be fine," she said, still letting him know she wasn't going to give up her independence.

As Jack got up from the log he was sitting on, Jasper came over to get one last pat on the head.

"Night, boy."

Jasper looked at Maggie as Jack's moonlit shadow went into the bush. Wanting to follow, Maggie told Jasper to stay. Jasper was becoming use to Jack being around. Maggie didn't think it would be a problem unless Jasper went to find Jack at his campsite. It was a good thing Jack brought the pail of water to her campsite after all. Now she had some water to put on the campfire before retiring for the night.

"C'mon boy, bedtime."

Maggie zipped up the tent once inside and got into her sleeping bag with Jasper taking his usual spot beside her.

What a great day after all, she thought, and a very nice evening too.

The rhythmic sound of the swaying trees put Maggie and Jasper into a deep sleep. Not a noise was heard from the creatures living within the park. Even the crickets were quiet tonight as the moon gently danced across the clouds that came in its way.

CHAPTER 4

Today Maggie and Jasper got up early. With the water Jack brought up from the river she was able to wash and use some to tame her unruly hair. Maggie thought she would rent a rowboat today and see how Jasper would like it. There would certainly be more room for him in a rowboat than a canoe. Down to the store Maggie and Jasper went. She took her fishing gear and worms as well as bottled water.

"Hi, Kim. I decided to rent a boat today. It's been a while since Jasper, and I have been in a boat and it's going to be a beautiful day."

"Sure, Maggie, one second, just on the phone with a client," said Kim as she moved her ginger-coloured hair away from her ear.

"Take your time, no hurry, Kim."

As Kim was on the phone Maggie decided to look around. Hmm...this looks good, Maggie thought, egg salad on rye. It's been a while since I've had one. Once you see it, you just can't unsee it. So now something special for Jasper. This will definitely be a treat. Chicken and bacon on whole wheat. That's a winner.

"Sorry, Maggie, a man wanted to book a campsite for two months next year."

"That's great, Kim. Always nice to have things booked ahead of time so you know how your year is headed."

"So true, so now what can I get for you, Maggie?"

"Jasper and I would like to rent a rowboat for the day, and I couldn't pass up these two sandwiches. I haven't had an egg salad sandwich in a long time. I just never think about making one, looks yummy too."

"Great, Maggie. Here's the key to unlock the boat. It's the one with the red oars. You have it for the whole day so enjoy."

"Jasper and I will be going home tomorrow, Kim. Here's my card, might as well pay for everything now."

"Thanks, Maggie. Too bad you're not staying longer. You never take much time off and I don't see you too often," said Kim.

"I know," said Maggie. "Maybe next year. I'll lock up the boat and drop off the key in the door mail slot when I bring it back, so you won't have to worry about it. I know your closing early today."

"Have fun, Maggie, bye Jasper."

"Bye, Kim, enjoy the rest of your day."

Maggie and Jasper made their way to the dock. There were a few boats missing from the dock. But the one with the red oars really stood out among the ones still sitting there. You couldn't miss it. The oars looked brand new.

"In you go, Jasper. Sit boy."

Maggie put in the fishing gear, worms and bottled water. Next, the sandwiches she bought from Kim. She unlocked the padlock that was connected to a cable holding the boat in place at the dock. Then, she got in, slow and easy was today's motto. They had all day to enjoy. On went the life jacket that was under the seat. She put the oars into the oarlocks and left them inside the boat. Then she unhooked the ropes from the boat and pushed herself away from the dock. Maggie lowered the oars into the water while Jasper was sitting in the stern of the boat watching the dock and the store disappear as Maggie rowed onward. Now that she was far enough away from shore, she stopped rowing to put a worm on her hook. The water looked like glass, not a ripple anywhere. Again, it was a perfect day for fishing and Jasper was enjoying the rowboat, taking it all in.

How beautiful the shoreline looked as she continued rowing. You truly get a different perspective with all the trees brightly coloured. The yellows, oranges and reds are amazing, Maggie thought. It was a mirror effect around the whole river. What a beautiful sight. She could also see each individual campsite that was nestled within the trees. Some still had their campfires burning, probably cooking breakfast.

"Well, Jasper, it won't be long now," Maggie said, as she stopped rowing.

Maggie bent over to retrieve her fishing box she had put under the seat. Opening it, she was looking for her fishing rod holder that she always carried. It had a clamp on it, so you could attach it to almost any boat. She decided if she was going to row, she might as well cast her line into the water and troll fish. In the line went, then placing the handle into the rod holder. The boat would be moving quite slowly but trolling none the less.

Her dad loved trolling. He took her to Peer Lake one year, specifically for trolling. On Peer Lake you could use motorboats. The number of rainbow trout and largemouth bass they caught within hours of their first day was unheard of. Sad really when you think about it, five rainbow trout and three largemouth bass. Just imagine if everyone who fished there caught that many fish in only a few hours, she thought. There would be nothing left to catch, thank goodness there were limits. The Fisheries and Wildlife Departments did however, stock the lake each year. So, she was sure the lake wouldn't run out of fish. Her dad put most of the fish he caught back into the water. Two fish were enough to cook a nice meal, he always said, but if one fish was big enough for two, then one would do.

There was a lodge on the lake too. They stayed there a few times because of the derby they ran. It was quite exciting for the fishermen. People came from all over, just to get their names added to the trophies with their picture hanging in the General Store at the lodge. The biggest rainbow trout and the biggest largemouth bass won the title. The year that Maggie and her dad went, one guy won both. Yes, it was her dad. It was the greatest derby ever and something Maggie will never forget. Maggie paused from rowing as she saw her rod bending.

"Look boy, either I have a fish, or I'm snagged."

Maggie stopped rowing and brought the oar up and into the boat. Just in case she had a fish she didn't want the oar getting in the way of bringing it into the boat. Slowly she reeled in her line. Jasper was waiting patiently to see if there was a fish. The line was a long way out, but Maggie was able to reel it in, so it must be a fish she thought. Then, yards away from the boat a fish jumped.

"Look, Jasper, that's ours," Maggie called.

Finally, she reeled it all the way in and placed it into the boat. It jumped so much Jasper went over and put his paw on it. This fish wasn't getting away.

"Shall we try for one more?"

Jasper barked, letting Maggie know to try for another one. Maggie took out the snap chain stringer from her fishing box and secured the fish. Over the boat she lowered it into the water keeping it fresh until they went in; making sure the other end was latched onto the boat. After baiting her hook again, she tossed her line back into the water and then she placed the oars into the water as well. Maggie was getting hungry and had been eyeing that egg sandwich all morning. It must be the fresh air she thought. She opened Jasper's first and broke it into pieces and laid it on the seat.

"Take it slow, boy," she said petting his head.

Maggie knew Jasper would eat it in one big bite, unless she told him to eat it slow. This was a very big treat for him, and he would devour it quickly.

"Good boy, Jasper. Here's a drink to wash it down."

Maggie used the plastic container that Jasper's sandwich was in and poured some bottled water into it for Jasper to drink. He took a drink then curled up on the floor of the boat, letting Maggie know it was time for a snooze.

Maggie finally opened her sandwich. She sat back and let the boat drift, although the river was still calm, it hardly moved at all. Her line was probably on the bottom of the river now, waiting for any fish to steal her worm.

"Oh my, this is so good," she said. "Kim knows how to make a great egg salad sandwich."

So quiet and peaceful, Maggie thought. No motorboats, was probably one of the reasons. But more than that, people respected the campgrounds and the wildlife within its boundaries. Everyone came here for the same reason, quiet and relaxation. The sun's rays from in between the clouds were dancing on the water, teasing the dragonflies passing by. Towards the shoreline Maggie saw an area of water lilies. It was a marshy area that fish are known to hide in. Hmm . . . she thought, why not. She brought in her fishing line and saw that her worm was still hanging on. Over the boat she threw her line. It landed just under some of the water lilies. Now we wait and see.

Jasper had awakened from his sleep all refreshed, patiently watching a spider that had made a web in the corner of the boat. Up and down the little guy went weaving in and out. This tiny spider was making a web to catch its dinner, something Maggie could relate to. Maggie's line had pulled slightly, hardly bending the rod. It can't be a fish, she thought, the rod would be bending more. It could be the movement of the boat, but the river was still calm. Jasper took his eyes off of the spider and began watching Maggie.

"What do you think, boy, time to reel in?"

Maggie began reeling in, now it was the second thing she thought it was, yep, she was stuck. Her line was hooked on the water lilies or other plants at the bottom of the riverbed. Now what, she thought. She decided to reel her line all the way in, pulling the boat alongside of the water lilies. The more she reeled in, the closer the boat got to the end of her line. Now with the boat beside her line she got up and bent over the boat to retrieve it. Pulling and pulling it by hand, while Jasper looked on patiently at what Maggie was doing.

"It's really stuck, Jasper; I guess I could cut it."

Maggie still bent over gave her line one more big pull.

"Need any help, Maggie?"

As she tugged hard on the line, she heard Jack's voice. Her line gave way, and Maggie fell backwards into the boat. Again, so embarrassed, she told Jack she had everything under control. The only good thing at that very moment was that her worm was still on her line. Why was he everywhere she was? Was he now becoming a stalker? Everything just seemed too coincidental. Looking behind her she saw Jack in a canoe.

"Hi Jack, you startled me. My line was stuck, and I decided to try and pull it out, instead of cutting it and leaving it in the water."

"I saw that," chuckled Jack. "I just thought I could be of some assistance. But I see you handled it yourself."

"Yes, I did, but thank you Jack," said Maggie abruptly. "I just don't like cutting the line because it can harm the waterfowl or other animals living on the water. If a fish takes the worm and eats the hook, then a loon or seagull eats the fish, then the bird now has a hook in it. It's just not good for the wildlife. Have yourself a nice day, Jack," said Maggie trying to explain herself. "Nice to know there's always someone watching," she said under her breath.

"And you too, Maggie."

Jasper was glad to see Jack. Wagging his tail and barking at his presence. He even wanted to get into Jack's canoe.

"Another time, Jasper," said Jack.

Jack paddled his canoe down the river and onto shore, as Maggie and Jasper watched on. All the while Maggie shaking her head, "men" she would say under her breath. There was something about that man that irritated Maggie. Maybe it was because he was always there at the wrong time, and to think he was going to take Jasper for a canoe ride. So condescending, she thought.

Once she calmed down, Maggie decided to row away from the water lilies, since the worm was still on her hook that meant there were probably no fish to pursue. Either way she wasn't going to take another chance of getting her line stuck. She rowed back into the middle of the river and decided to row in the direction of the store. It was starting to get late in the day. This was her last chance to catch another fish for supper. Maggie put a fresh worm on her hook and cast her line away from the rowboat. Rowing back to shore she decided to think of the journey home tomorrow and not think about Jack. As upset as she was, she was not going to let it wreck her and Jasper's last day.

They were almost at the dock and Maggie thought they would have only one fish for supper. Then a big splash was heard a few feet away from the boat.

"Wow, Jasper, look!" yelled Maggie.

Maggie grabbed her rod and reeled in her line as quickly as she could. So excited, she just wanted to get it into the boat, no playing with this one. The fish came along side of the boat. She pulled it up and over. It hit the bottom of the boat and looked at Jasper, eye to eye. A good-sized bass, probably the largest Maggie has caught while on this trip. So excited and proud of the catch, she realized she could have caught it at the end of the dock. The boat was only a few feet away. She positioned the boat into its space at the dock. Her boat was the only one left to come back. She removed the oars from the oarlock and placed the oars into the boat.

With the fish still in the boat she pulled her stringer out of the water. She opened a latch and put it into the gill and through its mouth and closed it again. Two beautiful fish, she thought. Well worth the wait.

"Come, boy, up on the dock," said Maggie, holding the boat in place for Jasper to get out.

Maggie, still in the rowboat tied the ropes connected to the dock back onto the boat to secure it in place. She took off her life jacket and put it under the seat. She put all the fishing gear on the dock beside Jasper and gave Jasper the sandwich containers, one inside of the other.

"Hold on to these, boy."

Then out of the boat she stepped. Now she had to connect the cable to the boat and close the padlock. Reaching down inside the boat she lifted out the fish on the stringer.

"Can't forget these," she said.

Maggie took one last sip of water and placed the empty bottle under her arm. She then picked up the fishing gear and stringer and headed down the dock to the store.

"This way, boy, put it in here. Good boy, here this one too," she said, giving Jasper the plastic bottle.

Kim always kept a big empty oil drum for garbage at the end of the dock. She knew people would have garbage to throw away when they got back to shore. After all she sells sandwiches and munchies to the campers. Plus, it stopped people from throwing garbage in the river. The signs posted everywhere telling people of the fines didn't hurt either. One last thing to do and that was to put the key into the mail slot in the door.

Tired and hungry, Maggie and Jasper went back to camp. Maggie put the last of the wood into the fire pit. She lit it and the snapping of burning wood was intermittent. Soon there would be a steady flame, which gave her time to fillet the fish. Jasper was again off doing his thing. He was running between trees in pursuit of a squirrel that had caught his eye. The squirrel actually wanted Jasper to play with him. The squirrel was running to a tree going a few feet up and down again, then running across the ground to another tree. Jasper thought it was a game and was happy to play. Every once in a while, the squirrel would stop and look at Jasper. Jasper would bark as if to say keep going. Maggie just smiled to herself.

Maggie had finished cooking the fish and plated them and was waiting for them to cool off.

"Say goodbye to your friend, Jasper," said Maggie, "time to eat."

Jasper barked and then came running. Maggie again smiled to herself. She loved him so much.

It was time for coffee, but it was instant tonight. She wondered if she would have another visitor. Maggie and Jasper sat by the campfire, again looking into the night sky. Maggie's mind kept rehashing the events of the day. She still couldn't believe Jack saw her in the state she was in. Too tired to think about it anymore, Maggie decided to turn in. There was still water in the pail that Jack had brought up the day before. Maggie poured it on the campfire.

"C'mon, Jasper, bedtime."

Into the tent they both went, Jasper taking his usual spot.

"Night, boy."

CHAPTER 5

The rustling of the trees could be heard throughout the campsite. The sky overcast, bringing with it heavy rains. All the creatures were hidden within their homes waiting for it to pass. The wind had picked up speed now and a big crack of thunder had shaken the earth, as the pouring rain drenched everything in its path.

"It's okay, Jasper. It's just a storm."

It had to rain sometime, but why now? Maggie thought. It could have at least waited until the car was packed. She checked her watch, and it was six forty-five; not really the time she wanted to get up. Maggie was still tired from yesterday. But all in all, the last few days were great. Fishing was good and each day warmer than the last. The strong wind was shaking the tent as Maggie carefully unzipped it to look outside. Holding tightly onto the door flap Maggie could see the trees swaying back and forth and the wind was blowing the rain sideways. The heavy rain snapped the fall leaves off the trees and onto the ground. They were flying everywhere. The noise of the rain pelting against the tent was scaring Jasper. Braving the wind and rain Maggie got her car keys and unlocked the doors.

"Jasper, come boy, get in."

Into the car Jasper went, Maggie closing the door behind him. This way Jasper was safe, and

Maggie didn't have to worry about him. Maggie gathered her fishing gear, water pail and cooking pan and put everything into the hatchback of her car. Any food like bread, granola bars and Jasper's kibble was always left in the car in case of wildlife coming to their campsite looking for food. Maggie was drenched now and went to get her sleeping bag and clothes from inside the tent. She threw them in the back seat while Jasper was sitting in the passenger seat looking wide eyed at Maggie.

"Good boy, almost done," Maggie said, patting his head.

Maggie closed the car door and went to take down the tent. She stepped into a puddle then slipped and fell into the mud. Picking herself up Maggie went over to the tent and removed the pole from inside, letting the tent collapse to the ground. The ground was so soft with all this rain all she did was pull the pegs out by hand. She realized with the ground being so wet and the pegs not secure, the wind could have blown the tent into the trees or another campsite. Maggie rolled up the tent and put it into the hatchback. She stood in the rain for a few minutes, letting the rain shower the mud off of her. Now thoroughly drenched, she got into the back seat, closing the door behind her. In her bag of clothes, she had her towel. Maggie undressed and dried herself off and put on yesterday's clothes. It really didn't matter as long as they were dry. She would take a shower when she got home. So glad to have everything in the car, they were ready to leave. She climbed into the front seat,

Jasper wagging his tail excessively, so happy to see Maggie next to him.

"Let's go home, Jasper."

Maggie started the car, the rain still pouring down. Luckily, she had parked on the stone pad provided for the campers instead of parking close to the campfire. The car might have been stuck in the mud by now. The sky was still cloudy, and Maggie didn't think it was going to stop anytime soon. Thankfully her campsite wasn't too far from the road leading out of Carleton Falls State Park. A few more turns and she was on the road heading home.

She was glad she was leaving today. Staying in a tent most of the day while raining outside would not have made for a great day. Hmmm, something to think about in the future she thought. Maybe a camper might be a better idea next time. Pop it up and pop it down and if it rains, we stay dry. That was something definitely to think about. But then again, her dad would have never used a trailer. It was his way of being with nature, roughing it. Maggie really missed her dad.

The wipers of the car were on high, back and forth, back and forth they went. It was really hard to see the lines on the road. Thankfully there was a truck up ahead, and Maggie could see its taillights through the downpour. She was hoping she could follow it to town. If she had brought her phone, she could have looked to see what the weather forecast was. They could have left last night and avoided it all together. All she could do was enjoy the ride home, another forty-five minutes to go she thought, as the weather was slowing down traffic, a half-hour drive it wasn't going to be. Maggie, being impatient though and maybe a little bored started tapping her fingers on the steering wheel. She remembered the song her and her dad used to sing.

The air is fresh and crisp tonight, As we sit and wait for the bass to bite, We hold our rods nice and tight, To steady the catch that's in our sight. Then a splash, so big and loud, Making this fisherman so proud, A largemouth bass on the end of the line, Soon to make a meal that's fine.

It was a song that they made up for the drive. They would look out into the beauty of nature and anticipate the catch as they were driving and singing their song. With the car window up Jasper couldn't amuse himself with his head stuck out the window. He listened attentively to Maggie singing the song as he curled up on the passenger seat. They would be home in no time.

"Oh no," cried Maggie.

The highway had slowed down, with the traffic coming to a crawl. Maggie looked at her watch. It was already nine-fifteen. It had taken her longer to pack than she thought. Oh well, in another half hour they should be home. She couldn't wait to take a shower and eat. At least her hair looked pretty good; the rainwater made her curls nice and soft. It was still raining hard and if the traffic didn't start to move a bit quicker it would take her even longer to get home.

She noticed a car pulling a camper, going the other way on the highway. Probably going to the park, she thought. Then she wondered where Jack was. He must have gotten rained out too, along with the rest of the campers. Maybe he wasn't a stalker after all, or he would have been at her campsite to say goodbye. Thinking of all the times he saw her, in her not so wonderful state and him being so arrogant trying to make it look like she wasn't capable of camping; that she needed a man in her life. She wouldn't have to worry about that anymore. She wouldn't be seeing him again. As she drove, her mind would drift, remembering how his dark brown hair moved in the wind. Every once in a while, he would take his hand and put it through his hair, taking it off his brow. His arms big and strong, probably from all that canoeing he does. He probably packed up and headed home too.

Traffic was moving a little quicker now. Maggie was now thinking of Magpie, hoping that everything went well while she was gone. There were a few big orders that they had to get out and her employees were quite capable of doing it. At times they would tell Maggie, you need to go on vacation. She just couldn't leave the business very often. She had to have her hands in everything and rightfully so because she had built this business from scratch.

Maggie was a wonderful baker, because of her grandmother, but as she got older, she decided that there was more that she wanted to learn. Her mother had encouraged her to go to baking and pastry school. Her grandmother had always made baking fun and that stayed with her all these years. You have to enjoy what you're doing otherwise you won't keep doing it. Her bakery was everything to her. With the baking knowledge and techniques that the school taught her, plus her grandmother's recipes and her ambition to create new ones, she became a world class baker.

But everything wasn't rosy at the beginning, either. When Maggie decided to sell baked goods, she made them from her kitchen. She put flyers out on car windows and bulletin boards in the stores to see if there was an interest in people wanting to buy baked goods. She knew probably there would be because there wasn't a bakery in Carleton Falls. But rather than spend money on a store she felt it was better to test the waters first. She started out selling mostly cupcakes and birthday cakes. A nice little business for sure but Maggie wanted to show more of her talents. She then decided to speak to the two catering businesses in town, giving them a price list of the desserts she would make. Both catering businesses decided to go with her because it gave them more time to focus on other parts of their business. The one catering business wanted to expand into wedding planning, which would also be a big plus for Maggie if they wanted her to make the wedding cake and desserts for the reception. This would be a lot of work for one person but could be very profitable as well. It turned out that she was way busier than she even imagined. She definitely needed to open a store. Her kitchen just couldn't handle it anymore, plus she needed to hire someone to help. She could make the baked goods but needed someone to take care of the customers and phone orders. Maggie needed to get the right spot for her business. She had first looked at a spot near Katie's Bed and Breakfast. It was a little small, but the rent was low, which was a good incentive to rent it, but her idea someday was a large beautiful bakery. Plus, she had some money put away that her grandmother left her. She really wanted to buy a store instead of renting. It would make her feel more accomplished.

She went into town one afternoon to Town Hardware. It was named after two brothers with the last name Town, Billy and Henry. The name of it couldn't have been any better if it had been planned. They are the only hardware store in Carleton Falls. So needless to say, they were usually quite busy. While passing the jewellery store, Lockmore Jewellers, Maggie headed to get a coffee at the Quick n Sip. There were no cars out front, which was very unusual; they were always busy. She pulled in and saw a sign on the door. It was a for sale sign, and they were selling it privately. Maggie got out of her car thinking it would be perfect for her bakery. Looking inside the store window, she saw a counter and a showcase that they used for donuts. Perfect for showing her baked goods and she could sell her grandmother's perked coffee. They even had tables and chairs, so the customers could stay and eat her pastries. It was perfect, the size of the store and the parking lot. This was her chance to have her own business.

Maggie had no time to lose. She called the number on the sign. It was owned by the Litmann family. Strange that Maggie didn't know they were going to sell; but then she had been pretty busy. She did hear from a customer that Lynn Litmann was ill. Maybe that's why.

"Hello, Mr. Litmann, it's Maggie Sinclaire. I'm interested in buying your business, would it be a good time to meet."

"Yes Maggie, nice to hear from you. Can you come over now?"

"Sure, Mr. Litmann, I will be over in fifteen minutes."

Leaving Mr. Litmann's home, Maggie was so happy. She was buying the coffee shop, with all the contents in the building. The money she got from her grandmother would finally be used to buy the store. She was so excited. It was the perfect location and the property in the back parking lot was all fenced in separating the property from the backyards of homeowners on the street behind. She was so happy that she decided to come into town. Someone else may have wanted to buy it. She needed to talk to Mr. Litmann's lawyer and finalize the sale as soon as possible. It only took a few weeks, and Maggie was the new owner of the old coffee shop. The shop came with a large walk-in cooler and a freezer, plus cooling racks. Maggie wanted special ovens and commercial mixers put in. She also needed an electric and a manual dough sheeter, for rolling dough.

A week before opening, Maggie came with Jasper to check the fencing around the property to see if anything needed to be repaired. Jasper as usual had found something to pique his interest. He was impressed with a grasshopper and its jumping abilities, trying to get to the grassy area it came from, between the fence boards. Jasper was going to make it his mission to help it out or at least guide it in the right direction. From one of the backyards that adjoined the property Maggie could hear a dog yelping and pushing on one of the fence boards, so persistently. It was definitely in a state and wanted to get through the fence and it wasn't going to stop. The board was being pushed and pushed until it fell off the main structure and through the fence came a dog barking and running towards Jasper. It was a miniature schnauzer that ran right up to Jasper then stopped barking. It immediately calmed right down and attentively started watching the grasshopper as well. It was the strangest thing Maggie thought that Jasper could have such a calming effect on another dog. Even Jasper didn't seem concerned about the dog. It was like they'd known each other for years. The owner of the dog walked around from the next street to talk to Maggie and apologize for what happened. Her name was Flora Kandale, a petite, older lady with a slight British accent. She told Maggie that a good friend of hers had passed away and this was her dog Tilly. She didn't want to see Tilly go to just anyone because she was such a handful, a very nervous, anxious and high energy dog. She would shred paper or anything else she could get her teeth on, just for the attention. After seeing Tilly with Jasper and how calm she was, Flora asked Maggie if she could watch Jasper while she was at work each day, then Tilly would have a playmate or teacher, and Jasper would be well looked after while Maggie was working. Flora offered to have the fence repaired but Maggie said not to worry about it as she would have a gate put in so she could drop Jasper off from the parking lot. This would be much more convenient for everyone. Flora invited Maggie to her house for coffee and they both watched in amazement at the behavior of Tilly. Maggie said she would bring Jasper by each day before the bakery officially opened for business. This would give everyone a rehearsal as to what it would be like.

Her mother and a few friends helped Maggie get the store ready for customers. They helped clean and painted the walls a pretty, light mint. Maggie had always found it to be a relaxing colour and it reminded her of peppermint and chocolate. She painted the front doors red, and it didn't take long for the sign company to put up the sign she'd ordered. It was a beautiful yellow with black fancy writing. They placed it right above the doors. Magpie Bakery was born and open for business.

"We're home, boy," said Maggie, as she now pulled into the driveway.

Jasper sat up looking out of the window. The rain had finally stopped, and the sun was trying to peek between the clouds. Maggie could unload the car without having to do it in the rain. Something to eat for her and Jasper would be nice too, then a nice shower, and clean clothes. She still wanted to drop by the bakery and see how everything was going. She was back in work mode now.

CHAPTER 6

Maggie and Jasper headed to the bakery. A lot of cars in the parking lot, she thought as she pulled into her parking spot. Maggie took Jasper through the gate to see Flora and Tilly. Tilly was jumping and barking as usual but as soon as she saw Jasper she was like a different dog, quiet and subdued.

"Have a good day Flora, I'll see you after work. Bye, boy, and you too pretty girl."

"Bye, Maggie, enjoy your day too."

Maggie went in the back door and into the back room as usual where she changed into fresh clothing. Then she would put on a clean apron and hairnet ready for a busy day.

"Hi, Maggie, you're back," said Julie, her number one baker. "Glad to see you, boss," she chuckled.

"Glad to see you too, Julie," said Maggie, tying her apron.

Julie and Maggie were best friends. They had gone through grade school and high school together. They looked a lot alike in height and build but Julie had brown wavy hair with blonde highlights throughout. A lot of their friends moved away after high school; being from a small town, they wanted to experience the big cities. Maggie loved Carleton Falls so much she would never leave. This was home. Maggie taught Julie the basics of baking and making pastries and Julie was a quick learner. Maggie always knew she could rely on Julie to supervise the other girls and run the business while she was away. Julie had married her high school sweetheart and both her and her husband always wanted to stay in Carleton Falls. Her husband Will, became a writer for the Hainesley Golden Gazette. After high school he took a writing course at college and landed a top position with them. Julie became a stay-at-home mom, to their three kids, Sara, Mark and Todd. When Maggie opened her bakery Julie wanted to help her get started. By then Will was able to write from home, he had become their star writer. With him being home now he could watch over the kids and Julie could work on her dreams. Julie was happy to be working for Maggie. She loved baking, but didn't want the responsibilities Maggie had. Her job was fun and creative. At the end of the day, she could go home and not worry about the business. Maggie had that under control.

Ella and Liz were hired a short time after Julie. They had left the part-time jobs they had in town for full time hours at the bakery. Ella, very tall and slim, had a very dainty, cutesy way about her. She was very much a people person. Liz, on the other hand, was shorter and medium build, she took her job very seriously and was very particular in how she did things. Both girls got along so well you would think they were sisters. Maggie couldn't have hired two nicer girls. Like Julie they were definitely a valuable asset to the business.

Maggie went out front to look at the showcase full of baked goods. Beautiful, she thought. It was a tasty collection of chocolate, marble and white cakes, each with their own creamy icing. The cookies were melt-in-your-mouth perfection as well as the custard and cream pastries. Bagels, muffins and tarts also had a place in the showcase, along with the scrumptious pies Maggie was known for. Julie had done a great job as well as the other employees. She could now rest easy should she decide to take some more time off in the future.

"Hello, Mrs. Murphy," said Maggie, spotting her sitting by herself. "Alone today?"

"Hi, Maggie, glad to see you back dear. Everyone else should be here shortly. I came early to get some seats for all of us. Your bakery fills up so quickly for your delicious baked goods and don't even get me started on your coffee. You're going to have to put in a drive-thru just for your coffee."

Hmm . . . Maggie thought, not a bad idea, something to think about for sure.

"Well, thank you, Mrs. Murphy, you have yourself a great day."

"Thank you, Maggie, you too dear."

Mrs. Murphy was good friends with Maggie's mom Sue. When Maggie's dad, Walter, was ill he was at the Hainesley Hospital and Ellen Murphy was his nurse. That was very comforting to Sue and Maggie because they knew he was in good hands. Ellen did her best to try and make it a little easier for them.

When she told them that they should leave to get some deserved sleep, she would stay and be with him. She was on her own time and wanted to help the family out. Maggie and Sue had stayed with him for days in a row, taking turns sleeping in a recliner in his room. They needed to sleep in their own beds and come back refreshed. Ellen had seen this too many times and knew they would be a little stronger if anything happened to Walter. Thankfully when the time came Walter went quickly. He passed away in his sleep, peacefully. All the time Ellen spent with Walter, she was reliving the passing of her husband, Paul. She had lost her husband very early in life. They were only in their twenties, and Ellen never remarried. She put all her energy into her work and the people of Carleton Falls. For a few years after she retired, she would go into people's homes using her nursing skills and take care of the elderly. She always knew what to say to perfect strangers. After her visits you would think they were long lost friends.

She gave that up last year seeing that there were just too many other areas in town that could use her help. Ellen came to the bakery faithfully every Sunday after church, sometimes alone and sometimes with the ladies' auxiliary. It was their way of getting together and talking about the town's Halloween dance or the Christmas plays being performed at the church. The church had a bigger auditorium than the school, so it made sense to have the plays there. Also, the church choir was used as backup for the plays. She was also head of the PTA. Even though Ellen didn't have any children she thought it was important to know what was going on in the community and in the schools as well. She was involved in most of the groups in town including community care. If you wanted to know anything in town, Ellen was definitely the one to ask.

Ellen was one of the friendliest people you would ever want to meet, always so happy and upbeat. The only time she ever got upset was when her cat Misty got out of the house and climbed up the tree in front of the house. She was so upset and beside herself. Misty was an indoor cat, and Ellen didn't want anything to happen to her. She was a Russian Blue cat. Her fur was a bluish grey and her eyes a beautiful green, a very gentle and affectionate cat. The tree was quite tall, and Misty just had to go as far as she could. Ellen called the fire department hoping they would get Misty down for her. Unfortunately, from experience they suggested leaving the cat alone and it would eventually come down on its own. People walking on the sidewalk passing by the tree tried to coax Misty down. Everyone in town knew Misty had climbed the tree. She didn't know what all the commotion was about. She was quite happy watching the birds that were squawking at her to get out of the tree. On the third day, and it was a hot one too, Misty must have been quite thirsty. Down she came and sat on the front step waiting for Ellen to open the door and let her in. When Ellen saw Misty, needless to say she was elated. Misty never got out of the house again.

"Hey, Maggie, how was your camping trip? Did you catch any fish?"

"Hi, Stew. The fishing was great, can't complain. The weather was good too, not like this morning. Jasper and I had fun and most of the time it was relaxing. It's nice to see you."

"Thanks, Maggie, it's nice to see you too. Your baked goods are delicious."

"Thank you, Stew, I'm glad you like them. Have yourself a great day."

Maggie was almost going to mention the awkward times at the campsite but decided against it. When she thought of the camping trip, she couldn't help but think of Jack. She was hoping he was all right with the bad storm they had. She knew she would never see him again, but because she didn't say bye she would never know. Julie interrupted Maggie's train of thought by coming out front to get her.

"Katie is here to get the croissants. She wants to talk to you."

Maggie went to the baking area. There was a large hallway that led to a side door. In the hallway the staff would put the orders ready for pickup.

"Hi, Katie, everything okay?" Maggie asked, a little nervously.

"Well, Maggie, I'm kind of in a bind. I wasn't expecting more guests, and I will need more croissants and muffins as well. Do you think there is any way you can help me?"

"One second, Katie, I'll check with Julie and see."

"All our reserves have sold out, but I will bake some for you and drop them off on my way home. That way you will have them for the morning."

"Thank you, Maggie, I really appreciate this."

"You're welcome, don't worry about a thing. What do you think, two dozen of each?"

"Perfect, I will see you later, Maggie."

"Bye, Katie."

Well, there wasn't time to waste. Maggie went to get the frozen ones that were already proofed and ready to bake, from the freezer. They always made sure the croissants had their final rise before freezing them. This way they could go from freezer to oven. However, Maggie always let them sit out for fifteen minutes before baking them. Having to make croissants from scratch was a lengthy process and Maggie wanted to make sure she had some on hand. Into one of the large commercial mixers, she added the ingredients. Once mixed and formed into a ball, she divided the dough in half and put it into the walk-in for at least thirty minutes allowing the gluten to relax. The dough should remain cold throughout the process as well as the butter block. The butter block was a very thin rolled out layer of butter that was already prepared and in the walk-in for when it was needed. She took one of the dough balls from the walk-in and shaped it into a rectangle. Maggie put it through the electric dough sheeter. This machine rolled out the dough to the desired thickness and length, which came in very handy especially on busy days, saving stress on the upper body and wrists from using a rolling pin all day. Maggie put it through a few times to get the length she wanted which should be double the length of the butter block. On top, in the middle of the long rectangular piece of dough she placed the butter block, leaving equal amounts of dough at either end. Maggie then took the dough at either end and brought it over the butter block to meet in the middle. Then she pinched the dough together where the join was in the middle and around the outside edges. The butter block was now incased in dough and now the process of rolling it out, then folding it, would begin. Maggie rotated the dough and put it through the dough sheeter again and again, until getting the desired length. Next, she would bring both ends into the middle of the dough and then bring one end to the other folding it like a book. Then she would rotate the dough, putting it back through the dough sheeter multiple times, getting the length she wanted then folding the dough into thirds. In-between each folding process Maggie would put the dough into the walk-in to rest, keeping the dough cold. Lastly, rotating the dough she put it through the dough sheeter at a selected thickness for the final croissants. Once she had the length she wanted, Maggie cut the rectangular dough into triangles, stretching out each triangle by hand and rolling it from the straight edge to the pointed edge, then placing it pointed edge down on a pan. After forming them into a croissant shape, she would let them sit and rise in a cool area and then she would put them into the walk-in leaving them overnight. In the morning, they would be put into the freezer. The last batch seemed to go quicker as Maggie was working on it each time the first batch was resting in the walk-in. On a daily basis because the process took so long and other baking was to be done, they did it in two days letting the dough rest in the walk-in over night after the first or second fold.

While making the croissants the timer on the oven had gone off and Maggie put Katie's croissants on the cooling racks. This was a special feature she wanted on all her ovens. She would set the timer for each item cooking and when the timer went off the ovens would also shut off. To her that was a must. If they got very busy, she didn't want to have to worry about the ovens burning the baked goods. She didn't like wasting money. Throwing away burnt baked goods and remaking them was not profitable. Also, it was peace of mind knowing the ovens were shut off, but out of habit Maggie always checked to make sure they were off when closing the bakery.

Now she needed to make the muffins for Katie. All the ingredients for the muffins were ready and mixed. The muffin pans were already lined with baking cups; something Julie liked to do in-between her orders. When the bakery got really busy it was one less thing to do. Maggie scooped the mixture out and placed each measured scoop into a muffin baking cup. Into the oven they went, making sure the timer was on.

Maggie needed a break and went outside and sat on the back step bringing with her a bagel with cream cheese and a coffee. Just something else they made at the bakery. Bagels and coffee were a hit with her customers. It was getting late, and the bakery would be closing soon. Maggie had been working on the croissants all afternoon and would be staying a little longer as she would have to box and bag Katie's order, then drop it off. Glad she stopped to eat and recharge; Maggie was ready to go back in.

"Bye, Maggie, have a good night," said Ella and Liz as they were leaving.

"Bye girls, thanks, you too."

"I'll lock up, Maggie, see you tomorrow."

"Good night, Julie, say hi to Will and the kids." Maggie went to check the oven. All the ovens were off. The muffins were already cool as Julie had taken them out and put them on the cooling racks. This saved time for Maggie, for sure. She put the croissants into two, one dozen bags incase Katie wanted to freeze any. The muffins were also put into two, one dozen boxes.

She turned all the lights off except the ones over the showcase. It was time to get Jasper but first she would put the baked goods into the car. Maggie had a large plastic container in her hatchback, especially made for the baked goods she had to deliver to clients, making sure they stayed fresh and clean. Before she got into the car Maggie went to lock the back door then went to get Jasper at Flora's.

"Okay, Jasper, one stop before home; Katie's Bed and Breakfast."

CHAPTER 7

Maggie slept in and woke up to a beautiful fall day. Jasper was keeping himself busy chewing on one of his chew toys. September would soon be over, and the winter months would be heading their way. Maggie went to the kitchen to make coffee, Jasper following her.

"Here's your breakfast."

Jasper went right to his dish and slowly ate his food. No need to gobble it up, it was the same kibble he's had for years. Maggie made her way to the shower with her cup of coffee and left it on the bathroom vanity for when she was finished.

"Come on, let's go outside," she said to Jasper while putting on her shoes.

Maggie had been eyeing the leaves that were already piling up on her front lawn. There were two large oak trees that were only half clothed leaving the rest of their unwanted leaves scattered across the ground. She went to get the rake from the shed with Jasper dancing alongside of her. Maggie raked the leaves making a big leaf pile for Jasper. Back and forth, in and out he went. Maggie laughed at the fun he was having.

"Nice to see you two having fun. Great day for it," called Charlie from across the street.

"Thanks, Charlie, how are you? Did you get through the banana bread I made for you?"

"I'm good and the banana bread was good too. It was gone two days later. Jesse and Molly dropped by and I served it to them. They loved it," said Charlie as he made his way across the street.

"How are they, Charlie, I haven't seen them in a while. Sorry I missed them."

"They're doing quite well. As a matter of fact, they both graduated from college. Being twins you might think they wanted to pursue the same things, but as you know they are so different. So, their courses were geared to their particular interests. Jesse has just taken an internship with the Rawlens Company north of the border. He is hoping to be hired permanently after he is done with his internship. They are a big tech company with their hands in so many other companies. He told me there would be a great chance for advancement. Molly has been hired at the Hainesley Medical Building. She will be their newest x-ray technician. I'm so proud of them. My sister did such a good job raising them."

"Yes, they are great kids," said Maggie. "I'm so happy that each of them has found the next stage of their life that is right for them. It's so important to be happy in what you're doing. It makes you want to push that much further to exceed your goals. Good for them."

Jasper, all tired out, went to lie down on the mat in front of the front door. Now the leaves were scattered all over the place ready for Maggie to rake them into a pile again. Charlie went home and

Maggie carried on raking the leaves, Jasper too tired to join in.

Maggie was thinking of Charlie's sister Rachel. She was a single mother, raising twins on her own. Charlie was always there for her and the kids. He was always a role model and a father figure for the kids and for Maggie too after her father passed away. She knew there was a lot more to his story than she would ever know.

She knew Charlie had never married. As the story goes, he had fallen in love with a girl in high school. They were making plans to be together. What he didn't foresee was his best friend falling for his girl and her for him. How sad for Charlie, she thought. But at that age how can anyone be certain if they are right for each other. The girl that he had fallen in love with was Maggie's mother Sue.

Charlie's friend was Walter, a tall, blonde, athletic type who made all the teams in high school. According to her mom, Walter made her laugh and made her feel special. Charlie did too, she would say, but Walter just captured her heart more. She really loved both men. Maggie was glad Walter was her father. Growing up she saw Charlie as a father figure too. After all Charlie was her dad's best friend. Charlie had never held a grudge. Charlie and Walter remained friends up until the time Walter passed away. He even asked Charlie to watch over Sue and Maggie. Charlie said yes because all he ever wanted was for Sue to be happy. Sue always knew that Charlie was there for her.

Not able to come to terms with Walter's death, Sue left town after the funeral. She left the house to Maggie and went to live in Italy. Her parents had come here from a small town in Italy and moved to Carleton Falls when Sue was eight. They loved it here and finding everyone so friendly, it reminded them of home. They came here hoping to make a better life for their daughter. It was no wonder Maggie's grandmother Alice or a-Lee-chay as it is pronounced in Italian, was a great cook and baker. Her recipes were handed down through generations and now it was up to Maggie to carry them on.

Sue was having a hard time and thought different scenery might help her. She had lost two of the most important people in her life, her mother and her husband. Walter had helped her through the passing of her mother years before he got sick. But with everything she had gone through, it was just too much. She made sure Maggie was in a good state of mind before she left and even asked Maggie to go with her. But Maggie was home in Carleton Falls. Charlie told Sue he would watch out for Maggie and not to worry. Maggie was like the daughter he never had, and she considered Charlie family too. Sue has been gone five years now and calls Maggie twice a month to get caught up on things. She was really doing well and had opened a little boutique selling leather purses, gloves and scarves. The money she makes is more than enough to keep her going and even pay the rent. Maggie is very much a businesswoman like her mother.

As for Charlie, no one will ever meet a nicer guy. After his and Sue's relationship failed, he concentrated on his education. He went to Harvard and got a number of degrees, then became a big CEO of a computer software company. He was still single and missed Carleton Falls so much that he eventually moved home. He had saved a substantial amount of money and bought a house across the street from Sue and Walter and pretty much became Maggie's Uncle. If he could be in a little part of Sue's life, he was okay with that.

Charlie also opened the Carleton Falls Mercantile. He bought an empty building seeing that the town needed a general store. But not just any general store. This was a store that had everything, from chewing gum to sporting goods. He wanted a one-stop-shop kind of store. He saw people going to Hainesley, for all kinds of things, when they could buy it here.

It was a good time to open a store too, because the twins had turned fourteen and Charlie had them in the store working. They made up every excuse they could not to work: 'We don't feel well,' 'I have too much homework,' 'I'm sick today.' But Rachel and Charlie were always one step ahead of them. One time Charlie had to go into Hainesley for some supplies and Molly and Jesse were minding the store. Jesse decided to take a break and have a nap. When Charlie came back it was time to lock up. Molly had told Charlie that Jesse had left and didn't come back. As Charlie and Molly left, Charlie activated the alarm system. Later that evening

Jesse woke up and thought he better get home. He went for the door and the alarm went off. Stunned and not knowing what to do, he sat and waited. It was two o'clock in the morning and it only took a few minutes for a police officer to arrive. Jesse was talking to the police officer trying to explain his way out of this.

"I was busy stocking the shelves and lost track of time, officer."

Just then Charlie walked through the door. He knew exactly what happened. It wasn't the first time Charlie had caught him goofing off or sleeping on the job. Charlie was really disappointed in Jesse and Jesse knew it. From that day on Jesse made sure he was on time for work and made sure he did what Charlie asked him to do. He was a different kid and even rubbing off on Molly, as she was having more interest in the business too.

As the business grew Charlie also saw a need for a pharmacy. His store was so huge he put in an area where the people could get their prescriptions. In the Hainesley Golden Gazette he put a help wanted ad to hire a pharmacist. It didn't take long to get a reply, and the pharmacy was in business for the people of Carleton Falls.

James Peters was the new pharmacist. He wanted to get away from city life and felt a small town would be a good change for him. It wasn't long before Charlie had introduced Rachel to James, and they hit it off from the start. They ended up dating for a year and decided to get married. Jesse and Molly loved the idea as they really liked James a lot. It would be good for Rachel to finally have someone in her life.

Charlie had sold the Mercantile to Rachel and James four years ago and had made a very large profit on it, which in doing so he could retire nicely. He was the one who paid for his niece and nephew to go to college, knowing that Rachel and James wouldn't be able to afford the schooling because it would take a while for them to make a profit on the business.

CHAPTER 8

Maggie let Jasper inside while she carried on raking the leaves that were now everywhere. It was worth it to see Jasper having fun. She got a few paper leaf bags and filled the bags up. She filled three bags and put them at the curb for garbage day. Returning the rake to the shed she then decided to go in and change. Jasper was sleeping on his large fluffy dog bed. He was so tuckered out from playing in the leaf pile that he didn't even hear Maggie. She put some kibble into his bowl and gave him some fresh water. She needed to stop in and see Katie at the Bed and Breakfast. Katie wanted to talk to Maggie when she delivered the order last night, but it was too late. She told Katie she would drop by today. Maggie went across the street to Charlie's house and knocked on the door.

"Hi, Charlie, I was wondering if you wouldn't mind looking in on Jasper. I wanted to go to the bakery, and he is sleeping, just too tired to get up."

"No problem, Maggie. I would be happy to."

"Thanks, Charlie, I shouldn't be too long."

"Take your time, if he's up I might bring him over here. This way we'll keep each other company."

"Thanks again, you're the greatest, oh, and here's the key. Bye, Charlie."

"Bye, Maggie."

Maggie could have asked Mrs. Abigail to watch Jasper as well but her car wasn't in her driveway. She figured Mrs. Abigail was with her friends playing cards. Each person in the group would take turns hosting the game in their home. Maggie was lucky to have such nice, friendly neighbours. Maggie called Flora to let her know that she wouldn't be around with Jasper today and that she would see her tomorrow. Flora laughed as Maggie was explaining about Jasper jumping into the leaf pile and too tired to get up. Flora was now thinking that maybe Tilly might like it too.

Maggie started her car and headed to Katie's Bed and Breakfast. The bed and breakfast was built on land where an old mill once stood. Katie had inherited it from her grandmother as she had inherited it from hers. A creek on the property cascaded over a rock formation to a stream below. The elevation of the creek was not too high above the stream, so the falls was more of a cascading waterfall, which in turn flowed into the Soul River. Maggie always thought it should have been called Bass River.

Maggie pulled into the bed and breakfast driveway and parked her car. She went to the side door as not to bother the guests coming and going at the front door. Going inside she spotted a, tall, slender, dark-haired man, quickly sweeping the hallway.

"Hi, Tony, how are you, it's been a while," she said, while giving him a big hug."

"I'm great, Maggie, just a little busy that's all. I'm a little overwhelmed these days."

Tony was the do all guy and Katie's husband. He carried luggage, washed dishes, did odd jobs, made beds, cleaned tables and even showed people to their rooms. Tony was a quiet, somewhat shy person who liked to be the one behind-the-scenes. Katie on the other hand was outgoing. Her stature was that of a model with long straight black hair. Her smile was captivating, as were the two dimples that went along with it. Tony and Katie were opposites for sure, but they complimented each other nicely. They were a perfect match.

"I'm not sure why we are so busy. People are coming and going so fast we barely have time to get the rooms ready. I'm not complaining … but yeah, I guess I am," he laughed. "I would rather be busy than not."

"I know what you mean. We're either too busy or too slow. We just want the in-between busy. Where is your beautiful wife?"

"I wish I could say Katie is resting with her feet up, but she is in the kitchen making homemade soup for supper tonight. Maybe you can put some sense into her head. With over a month to go, she should be relaxing. I'm sure when the baby is born; she will be a going concern like her mother."

"I'll see what I can do, Tony, you take care."

"You too, Maggie."

Maggie went down a wide corridor to a room off to the side. There was Katie over the stove stirring a big pot of soup.

"Yum, smells good."

"Oh! Hi, Maggie, I'm glad you're here."

"So, what was so important, Katie?"

"Well, first Maggie, you know I love you, right?"

"Yes, but you're scaring me, Katie. Is there something wrong? Are you and the baby all right?"

"Yes, we're fine. It's good news, for all of us, kinda."

"Okay let me have it, Katie."

"Well on November fifteenth I'm hosting a luncheon where people come to make a small pre-Christmas Yule log with a prominent baker showing everyone how to make their own small Yule log."
Maggie didn't know whether to laugh or cry at what Katie just said. It was a great idea, but the work involved with people making cakes, not to mention cooking those cakes, was a bit problematic. Maggie's mind was just spinning.

"How many people are we talking about Katie?"

"Well, so far, I have thirty people signed up already. I know what you're thinking. I should have asked you first. A few people I talked to thought it was a great idea and wanted to be a part of it but then they told their friends, and here we are."

"I know you're helping me as well," said Maggie, "and I thank you. So, let's top this off at thirty-five and no more. Let me know whether you want croissants, rolls or fancy bread for sandwiches. As for the small Yule logs, there isn't enough oven space to accommodate all the cakes. So, I will make thirty-five cakes the night before, because they need to be very fresh so the people can unroll them. On the day of the event, I will show the people how to make a Yule log from scratch, so they can make one at home. They will have a cake in front of them ready to be decorated. While my cake is cooking, it would probably be a good time to have your sandwiches for your luncheon. After mine comes out of the oven, I will show them how to roll and then unroll the cake and add the filling. Then they can unroll the cake in front of them and add the filling as well. Then we will roll our Yule logs back up and cover them in chocolate icing. The last thing to do is decorate. I will bring the icing and filling in a big bowl and spoon some into small containers for their Yule log. I will also bring decorations for the cakes. Julie can do the regular day-to-day baking and the orders, while I concentrate on the luncheon when the time comes. No more than thirty-five, Katie."

"Agreed," said Katie, "I knew you would be up for it."

She was so happy, hoping this might be a regular yearly thing.

"Yes, it's a great idea. Plus, I have been pondering an idea Mrs. Murphy had mentioned to me. She thinks my coffee is so good that I should have a drive-thru, this way people can get their coffee quicker. The extra money doing this luncheon just might make it possible."

"Thanks, Maggie, love you," said Katie as she gave Maggie a hug goodbye.

"Love you too and do Tony a favour and rest once in a while."

Maggie left by the side door and went to get into her car. The view was breathtaking. The land was beautiful; green valleys with fall-coloured trees everywhere. Spruce and evergreens were sporadically placed throughout. The echoing sound of the waterfall was so elevating to hear as well as beautiful to see. It was the first thing you passed by when entering Carleton Falls; just another reason why Maggie loved it here.

It was such a beautiful day, so Maggie decided to take the long way to the bakery. As Maggie turned a bend in the road, she noticed something along the grassy verge. It was a small dog sitting quietly watching the passing cars. She wondered what it was doing there and where it belonged. She knew she would be heart-broken if Jasper had strayed away. Maggie pulled up on the shoulder of the road and got out of the car. It was a beautiful, tan-coloured cocker spaniel. Maggie's grandmother had a black-coloured cocker spaniel named Riley. He was a very sweet dog with a great disposition that followed her everywhere.

"Come girl, I just want to see if there's a name on your collar. I'm sure someone is missing you." The dog seemed to welcome Maggie, as if she had been waiting for someone to come and rescue her. Maggie found a name and a number to call.

"Come girl, in the car."

Maggie opened the back door and persuaded the dog into the car, then closed the door. She went around and got into the driver's seat.

"Now to call your owner."

The line was busy, she waited and tried again.

"Hello, is this Mr. Sands?"

"Yes, it is."

"I just found your dog. She was sitting on the side of the road as I passed by."

"Kids, Mandy has been found," Maggie heard on the other end. "Thank you so much, where can I pick her up?"

"I'm on my way to Magpie Bakery. I will meet you there. Bye."

Maggie got back on the road and headed to the bakery.

"So, your name is Mandy. Well girl, I'm taking you to your family."

Mandy was lying quietly on the back seat. Who knows how long they had been looking for her. Rounding the corner Maggie pulled into the parking lot. Once out of the car she waited for Mr. Sands. She didn't want to let Mandy out just yet; she was still sleeping. About ten minutes later a car drove up and parked. A man went inside and came back out with a coffee and a bagel. A few minutes later another car pulled in. Maggie waited to see if this was Mr. Sands. A tall, medium build man with dark hair, wearing an overcoat, got out of the car.

"Are you Mr. Sands?" Maggie asked.

"Yes," said the man as he opened the back door of the car.

Out came two young girls maybe age eight and ten. As they were approaching Maggie's car, Mandy was barking and wanted to get out. Maggie opened the door and watched the touching reunion.

"I can't thank you enough, miss," he said. "It's been three days now and we didn't have much hope of finding her. She got out the back gate that I have been meaning to fix."

"I'm just glad I saw her, and everything turned out okay."

"Thank you very much and if there is anything I can do for you, please don't hesitate to ask," he said, leaving Maggie with one of his cards.

After waving goodbye Maggie glanced at his card. Sands 'n Sons Construction, in Hainesley. He must be one of the sons of the owner, she thought. She put it in the glove box just in case she ever needed it. He seemed like a very nice man and definitely happy to have Mandy back.

Now that the excitement was over, she went into the bakery. She headed to the showcase and waited on some customers, wanting to give Ella a break. She enjoyed talking to customers like Mr. Brown, a quiet yet well-spoken man. Every week he came in for the same thing. As soon as you saw him coming, you knew what he wanted; two vanilla slices. It was flaky pastry with custard between the two layers and vanilla icing on top. It was his favourite and he came the same day every week, buying two and only two. Julie always remembered to put two aside for Mr. Brown, we wouldn't want any disappointments. Then there's Jenny Smith, an older lady with dark rimmed glasses who comes in for Maggie's shortbread cookies. Her sister used to send her some from Scotland but has since left Scotland and is unable to get any for her. Jenny now comes to Magpie because Maggie's short bread cookies are just as good, maybe even better she says. And then there was Bill Rowan, a happy-go-lucky kind of guy that comes in for cream puffs. Not one or two but a whole dozen every Friday morning for his employees. He was a very pleasant, considerate man and the local real estate agent for Carleton Falls.

Her grandmother's recipe for perked coffee has been a big hit too. It's amazing how many people drink coffee. Some like it black, others with milk or cream and some prefer it with whipped cream. That's about as fancy as it gets, but people come for the taste. Too bad her grandmother hadn't known about this. She could have sold her recipe to the big companies. But just as well, now Maggie can keep up the tradition and keep it in the family.

All in all, it was a very busy day for Maggie. When she picked up Jasper from Charlie's he was so happy to see her. As much as Charlie was a good dog sitter, Maggie was his best friend.

CHAPTER 9

Magpie Bakery was keeping very busy. With the town Halloween dance soon approaching, Maggie was busy getting all the ingredients ready for all the desserts she would be making. After the bakery closed Maggie would pick up Jasper from Flora's and go into Hainesley for supplies. Julie, taking care of the shop during the day as usual, gave Maggie time to get things ready for the dance. Maggie offered to do this on her own but Ray Fletcher at city hall said there were contingency funds to pay for things that were for the people of Carleton Falls.

Maggie was happy to do it no matter what and she had a new pumpkin recipe she wanted to try out. She took care of the desserts while the ladies of the church auxiliary made the food. The church had a large kitchen in their basement. The ladies were known for making pierogies, cabbage rolls, sausages, soups and stews and their famous ribs and sauerkraut. They also made a fantastic red potato salad. No one ever went home hungry. Mrs. Murphy made sure of that. Anybody and pretty much everyone came to the dance and the ones that didn't dance came anyway, just for the food and conversation. It was a way of getting the grownups together, something special for them. It was always the Saturday before Halloween. This way the dance and festivities didn't interfere with the children and their Halloween activities.

The Church with the help of the ladies' auxiliary always put on a Halloween party for the kids. Hotdogs and pizza were on the menu, along with Maggie's cookies and cupcakes for dessert. The pizza was from Phil's Pizza Palace. Phil took over his parents' diner and made it into a pizza business instead. He also made all kinds of subs as well. As for the hotdogs, the ladies would get one of their husbands to cook them in the church parking lot on a barbeque.

The dance was held at Ted Mason's tree farm, where he held multiple events such as hayrides, the town Halloween dance, a Farmer's Market, and anything else that he could entertain. Like Katie's Bed and Breakfast, Ted's farm was handed down through generations. The history of his farm was quite amazing; Maggie always told him that he should write a book about it. Maybe next year he would say, too busy. Maggie is still waiting. Back in the day his farm was known for its apples and still is. He sells them to grocery stores all around the state. They are a hybrid between green and yellow apples; they really gave her apple pies a nice taste. She will be making some for the dance as well as apple strudel too.

Everyone at the dance will be wearing a costume. Maggie had worn the same costume for years and I think the people expected it as well. She would dress up as a barmaid, which was quite appropriate because she was the one handing out the punch.

"I'm so excited," Julie said, as she was helping Maggie box the desserts. "I have been waiting for this for months."

"What are you going as, the same as last year? What was it, oh, a witch?" said Maggie.

"Oh no, there were so many witches and pirate costumes last year, we couldn't find each other. Every pirate I ran into wasn't Will and every witch he saw wasn't me," Julie laughed. "I really don't like asking people if they're my husband. Will, is that you? I think we all got our costumes from the same company."

"Gee, that would be annoying," said Maggie.

"Remember Mrs. Rowen's costume last year, Maggie? She made both her and Bill's costume."

"Mr. Rowen didn't look too happy but was a good sport about it."

"Yeah," Julie replied, "I don't know what she was thinking, Mr. and Mrs. Humpty Dumpty. The bottom of the egg was so narrow, he could hardly move."

"They did look cute though, bobbling as they walked," Maggie chuckled. "I had never seen so many Raggedy Ann and Andy costumes either."

"Maggie, we need to have a contest for the best costume. That way people will get unique and different costumes. Costumes that stand out," stated Julie.

"Well, if that was the case last year, Mrs. Rowen and her husband would have definitely won. I wonder what she's making this year?" said Maggie.

"I think I will mention your best costume contest to Mrs. Murphy. She will get the ball rolling on that, for sure. I'll call her now, this way she can start on it if she wants to, before I see her this afternoon."

Maggie and Julie were making a lot of baked goods today for special orders, as well as keeping the showcase full for customers coming into the bakery. The morning and most of the afternoon had flown by. Maggie took her car to city hall to meet with Mrs. Murphy. Out of respect for Mrs. Murphy, Maggie never called her Ellen. She figured she deserved it after all she had done for people and their families. To Maggie it was showing respect, and she had lots of it for Mrs. Murphy. She was so proud to know her. Maggie and Mrs. Murphy were going to pick up all the decorations and take them to Ted Mason's farm. It was also their task to decorate the barn. They didn't have time to waste; the Halloween dance was at the end of the week. It wasn't only for Carleton Falls' residents, people from other towns or even the big cities would come. People that came from out of town to Katie's Bed and Breakfast knew about it and would be back to attend and stay with her again. It was a big deal, a very big deal.

"Hi, Maggie, good timing, Ray just got here, and he said he will help pack our cars."

"That's great Mrs. Murphy, we can use all the help we can get."

"Oh, I got right on it, putting out pamphlets about a costume contest. Having a contest was a great idea, Maggie. Thank Julie for me; I don't know why we didn't think of it years ago. I've had a lot of positive feedback. So much so that Jane from Lockmore Jewellers is going to donate something for the prize. This is going to be fantastic, and people are already asking what others are wearing. They're all trying to win the prize."

"Wonderful," said Maggie, "it's going to be our best one ever."

Maggie and Ellen went to meet with Ray inside the building. Before they got inside the doorway Ray and a few others were carrying the decorations outside. Ray was always thinking of others, his easy-going and pleasant nature made you feel relevant, no matter what the subject matter was.

"Hi, Ray," said Maggie, "nice to see you."

"Nice to see you too, Maggie. Just open the trunks and doors to your cars and we will have everything loaded for you," said Ray.

It only took them three trips and the cars were loaded and ready to go. Maggie and Ellen watched like ladies of luxury, all the while, knowing the work they had ahead of them.

"Thanks, Ray, this was a lot of help," Maggie said, getting into her car.

"We really appreciate it," said Ellen.

"Any time, and if you need some help, let me know and I can send a couple of people to help out," said Ray, as they were leaving.

It didn't take them long to get to Ted Mason's farm. Ted was busy in the back buildings getting his apples bagged and loaded to leave Carleton Falls for the big cities. When she called to let him know they were coming he told Maggie to just go to the barn and get started. They backed their cars up to the barn doors. This way they could unload, taking their time. The farm looked beautiful. The trees stood tall and colourful. Some trees were only half clothed in their leaves. The rest were on the ground giving the area a very rustic look. The bales of hay that Ted put outside the barn doorway also gave that rustic look. A string of lights would help the effect out here Maggie thought. They both got together and put up two strings of lights. Maggie plugged them in and Ellen, smiling, nodded her head. Ted also had pumpkins everywhere, as he grew them to sell at the farmer's market. His kids had even carved some for them as well. This was shaping up to be a beautiful event. The outdoors was perfect, now for inside.

Maggie and Ellen put up the lights inside before bringing in more decorations. Next the tables that had been delivered were up against the wall, as well as the chairs. All they had to do was put them where they wanted them and add tablecloths. The chairs were sporadically placed within the large barn. Ted also put some bales of hay inside the barn. These made good seats as well. There were wagon wheels and barrels, as well as old fashion butter churns. Ted had piled corn stalks outside for the girls to use too. The barn was looking really good for the dance. There was only one thing left to do, but that was coming the day before the dance. It was a stage for the band to play on. It would be set up at the back of the barn, giving a lot of room for people to dance. They both went and stood in the doorway and looked into the barn at the work they had done. It was beautiful. So happy with the way it looked they turned off the lights and shut the doors. Maggie could call Ted later and thank him for all he had done. They were both tired and said their goodbyes, Ellen going home and Maggie back to pick up Jasper. The bakery would be closed, and Flora would be waiting for her.

As Maggie knocked on the door, Flora greeted her and inside she went. Both Jasper and Tilly were having a nap, side by side.

"Hi, Flora, how was your day?"

"It was great, each day Tilly is becoming calmer and has less anxiety attacks. Jasper has been great for her. I can't thank you enough Maggie and of course, Jasper too."

"You're welcome, Flora. We're all helping each other, and Jasper has become fond of you and Tilly, and I have as well."

Maggie said goodbye and opened the car door for Jasper. Into the passenger's seat he went.

"Long day boy? You and Tilly are becoming good friends."

Jasper nudged Maggie to let her know he was glad to see her.

"I think we should pick up some food and head to Hainesley. What do you think, Jasper?"

Maggie was tired but she knew what she needed more was to get her mind off the business and just relax; she and Jasper were headed to Hainesley. Even the drive would take her mind off work. Tonight was for her and Jasper. Her last visit was to pick up some supplies for Magpie. Tonight, the skies were clear, and the road was quiet without much traffic. Hmm . . . what to eat, she thought. Yep, steak subs. Jasper could use a treat and steak was it. She didn't even have to get out of the car. They had a drive-thru, just like the one Mrs. Murphy talked about.

"Two steak subs, please. One plain bun with everything and the other whole wheat with double meat and no garnishes please. Plus, a black coffee and a cup of water please."

It didn't take long considering they cooked them fresh. She pulled into a parking spot and pulled Jasper's sub apart.

"Here boy, eat up, you deserve it."

She then opened hers and took a bite.

"So good," she said as Jasper was still eating his.

It didn't take long for both of them to finish their subs. Maggie gave Jasper a drink of water from the takeout cup and she took a sip from her coffee. Not as good as her grandmothers or the bakery, but it would do.

"Well, boy, one more stop," she said, with Jasper listening attentively.

Maggie drove up the road and made a few turns before she pulled into this big familiar parking lot that was full of cars. Jasper looked out the window, dogs everywhere and all different breeds too. Jasper, eager to get out of the car, barked as Maggie opened the door. Maggie had brought Jasper to this dog park before. It was a large fenced in area where owners unleash their dogs so they can run and play. Here Jasper could interact with other dogs. Sometimes Maggie would have to leave Jasper more than she liked, but she sure made up for it. This was his time to run and play and have fun and it also gave her a chance to talk to some dog owners. The conversations would probably be about their dogs but that was okay, Maggie loved to talk about Jasper.

Running to see Maggie was a tan-coloured cocker spaniel. Jasper was now around Maggie too as she bent down to pet the other dog. It was Mandy and her tail was wagging in recognition.

"Hello, pretty girl," Maggie said as she looked up to see Mr. Sands standing a few metres away. As Jasper and Mandy were getting acquainted, Mr. Sands approached Maggie.

"Hello Mr. Sands, nice to see you and Mandy. We never really introduced ourselves. I know your name from the card you gave me. I'm Maggie Sinclaire."

"Hello, Miss Sinclaire, our paths cross again. So nice to see you. Your dog is very nice, his name?"

"His name is Jasper," said Maggie.

"Nice name, Jasper, come boy," said Mr. Sands.

Jasper came over to greet Mr. Sands with Mandy following Jasper. The two dogs were really hitting it off. Mr. Sands knelt down to pet Jasper. Mandy, getting a little jealous squeezed right between them.

"It's okay girl, I still love you," he said to Mandy, giving her a pat too.

Now standing he turned to Maggie and said, "I hope you take me up on my offer one day, Miss Sinclaire."

"I thank you for your offer. It's strange how things or people come your way when you least expect it or when in need of something. I own Magpie Bakery where we met. I was thinking of putting in a drive-thru. I think the parking lot is large enough to handle the traffic, but not really sure. I would need some expert advice."

"When would you be thinking of doing the construction of the drive-thru?" asked Mr. Sands.

"I was hoping to have it finished by December. So, any time now, but is it even possible to have one?"

"Well, first things first," Mr. Sands said. "I will come by tomorrow and take a look. Shall we say around two o'clock? Then I can let you know if it is even possible, and we'll go from there."

"That's perfect, Mr. Sands," said Maggie, "see you at two."

Mr. Sands and Maggie parted ways. Maggie took Jasper to the car and off they went, heading home.

Jasper had lots of exercise running and even playing with Mandy. Maggie couldn't believe the odds of seeing Mr. Sands at the dog park. There are a few dog parks in Hainesley, and they both picked the same one. She didn't believe in coincidences. Someone must be watching over her.

CHAPTER 10

Everyone at the bakery was in high gear. Tonight was the Halloween dance, and Maggie had her hands full. The girls in the shop also tried to help Maggie when they could. Julie was a blessing for Maggie; she was very good at what she does. She was good at juggling the workload just like Maggie, but then again, she had a good teacher.

Maggie, taking out her new recipe for pumpkin tarts from the oven, glanced through the window to the parking lot. She couldn't help but think about the conversation that she had had with Mr. Sands when he came to look at the bakery. She couldn't believe it was all going to come together. There was enough room in the parking lot for customers to come into a drive-thru and the exit. Plus, it wasn't going to take up too much space from her parking lot either. The window for the drive-thru will be on the far wall from the customer serving area. If she was as busy as Mrs. Murphy said she would be, then she would have to hire someone especially for the drive-thru. She might have to put a coffee maker close to the window as well. Mr. Sands said he would take care of the permits and with any luck should be finished before Christmas. Mr. Sands is also doing it at cost because of her rescuing Mandy. The money she would be getting from Katie's Bed and Breakfast luncheon and the money she had saved up would pay for it nicely. She was so excited because everything was coming together.

"How are the tarts, Maggie?" asked Julie, "they smell wonderful."

"Don't they and they look good too," Maggie said endorsing her tarts.

Jasper would love the aroma, she thought, just like his cookies. Maggie always made what she called Jasper cookies. They were dog cookies containing peanut butter and canned pumpkin. Jasper loved them, maybe Tilly would too.

"I boxed the four cheesecakes and put them in the walk-in for tonight. I also did a count while in there: six apple pies, five lemon meringue pies, four marble cakes, four chocolate cakes, three white cakes, five dozen cream puffs, eight apple strudels, and your five dozen pumpkin tarts. Have I missed anything?" Julie said, now standing beside Maggie.

"Just the boxed Halloween cookies that are ready to go. They're a good backup if we run out of everything else. Mr. Mason should be here shortly with his refrigerated truck," said Maggie.

"One person out front is still eating. Do you want me to lock the front doors after he leaves?" asked Liz.

"Yes, Liz, thank you," replied Maggie.

They were all eager to get home and put on their costumes. No one knew what each other was going to be except for Maggie's barmaid costume. Everyone wanted to win the costume contest. After all, Lockmore Jewellers was giving out a prize.

Just as Liz and Ella left the bakery to go home Mr. Mason pulled into the parking lot and parked alongside the customer pickup area and honked his horn. A tall lean man with greying hair got out and opened up the back doors to the truck. Maggie and Julie said hello and thanked him for coming. Maggie also thanked him for all the things he gave her to decorate the barn with.

"Did you make enough, Maggie?" Mr. Mason chuckled, looking at all the boxes.

"I hope so, I made as much as last year, but you never know."

"I'm sure you have enough," said Mr. Mason, with a warm smile. "I'm going to park the truck at the back of the barn, and plug it in. Your desserts will stay cool, and you can get them from the truck when you need them."

"Thank you, Mr. Mason, I'll get there as soon as I can. I have to take Jasper home and change for the dance."

"Okay, see you ladies later," said Mr. Mason as he got into the truck and drove off.

"I will see you later as well," said Julie to Maggie.

"Bye, see you at the dance."

Maggie turned out the lights and locked up. She went to get Jasper as usual, taking a few danish pastries for Flora, and then driving home.

Pulling into the driveway she saw Charlie looking out his front window. Charlie was waiting for Maggie as she had asked him in advance to watch Jasper while she was at the dance. She could have asked Flora, but Charlie was closer to home especially if she got home late. Charlie had only been to one Halloween dance many years ago. It was when he was dating Sue. He didn't want to relive the memories, so he stayed home. He didn't mind watching Jasper if it helped Maggie. Maggie went inside to get some food for Jasper and off they went to see Charlie. Charlie opened his door and Jasper ran in, happy to see him.

"Thanks again, Charlie," said Maggie. "Now I need to get changed and get to the dance. Bye Charlie, bye boy."

"Any time, Maggie, have fun," said Charlie.

Maggie hurried home and took a quick shower. She towel-dried her hair and arranged her curls. Then she put on her barmaid dress that she had laid out on the bed this morning. Her hair was longer than it was last year when she wore the costume, so she decided to pin up her hair. She left two curls that streamed down each side of her face. That looks better, she thought. The mask was still lying on the bed. Not knowing if she was going to wear it, she took it just in case. Already to go, she grabbed her keys, locked the door and got into her car. Off to the dance she drove, anticipating a wonderful night.

It didn't take her too long to get to the farm. From the roadway she could see the light strings that her and Mrs. Murphy put up outside. The barn inside was all lit up too. She pulled her car behind the barn and saw the refrigerated truck. Mrs. Murphy's car was there too. It was too early to bring out the desserts. The meal would have to be served first. She went into the barn through the back door. Everything looked so beautiful. Everyone that was helping out was here waiting for the crowds to arrive. Another half hour and the people should be piling in. The band was setting up their equipment and the stage looked great. Maggie saw a cowgirl wearing a mask and with a slice of toast tied to each arm. Could it be Mrs. Murphy? Maggie wondered looking at her height. Mrs. Murphy was a tall woman but not that tall, but then the two-inch heels would account for that. She was just going to have to guess.

"Mrs. Murphy, is that you?" Maggie asked hesitantly.

"Why yes, Maggie," she chuckled, "do you know what I am?"

"A cowgirl, but I'm not sure about the toast."

"I'm a toasted western," she laughed. "Since I helped make the food, I thought a sandwich would be appropriate."

"You're just too funny, Mrs. Murphy. It's a great costume. You look really good."

"Thank you, dear and you as well."

"Thank you, Mrs. Murphy. Who's bringing the food?"

"Ray, that dear man, has so many connections. A truck is picking up the food and is bringing the two steam tables that we use at church functions. All we have to do is unload, plug in and we're ready to go. He's scheduled to be here in an hour. I'm so glad we decided to use the steam tables this year. It's going to be a lot easier."

People were starting to enter the barn. There was a mouse and a cat, a mummy, a ghost, a spider, a bee, a pumpkin, a dog, a vampire, and a frog. Not one costume was the same so far and everyone had a mask. How am I going to recognize anyone? Maggie thought. She couldn't believe Mrs. Murphy's costume. It was amazing but so out of character from her usual dressy casual attire. What an inspiring person Maggie thought, smiling to herself, she looked great in her costume and the idea was so impressive, just like the drive-thru idea. Maggie even wondered how she was going to find her friends. I guess they would just have to find her she decided, and on her mask went. The people helping at the door were in masks too. One was dressed as a hotdog, the other a cowboy. They were the host and hostess, welcoming the people as they arrived.

The band was giving the people a little hint of what was to come. They were a different band than last year and were supposed to have a wide variety of songs to get the crowd up and dancing. The first one was a square dance. There were a lot of people here already. The caller said to grab a partner. There was a doll dancing with a monster, a princess with a prince, a pumpkin and a gingerbread man, even the bee was dancing with the frog. The costumes were spectacular. It was going to be hard to pick the best one, and only one.

Maggie made sure she stayed at the punch bowl. All the bottles of fruit juice and soda pop were under the table. It wouldn't take her long to make more. The limes, lemons and oranges were already sliced and in a cooler with the ice cubes. Mrs. Murphy saw to that. Maggie filled the glasses and set them on the table. The guests just had to help themselves.

"Hi, Maggie," said a voice behind her.

Maggie turned to see who it was. Standing in front of her was a big puffy marshmallow and a cup of coffee standing beside her. The costumes were great. As the marshmallow was talking, Maggie was trying to figure out who it was. It was Katie and Tony. What a great way to hide her pregnancy.

"Your costumes are great, Katie," said Maggie giving Katie and Tony each a hug, "finally, two people I know. I can't tell anyone apart."

"Well, you didn't hear it from me, but you see the bee, that's Rachel and the frog is her husband, James. The butterfly is Liz and Ella is the mermaid."

"How did you find out?"

"You have to mingle Maggie, if I find out anymore, I will let you know."

Off Katie and Tony went to mingle some more. Maggie was getting the hang of it now. A ghost and a mummy came to get some punch, and Maggie said they had great costumes. While complimenting them she asked them who they were. She knew their voices but just couldn't figure it out. They made her guess. After the third chance they told her they were, the Town brothers Billy and Henry. Then everyone laughed. They told Maggie they were really enjoying themselves and pointed out their wives to Maggie. The fairy was Billy's wife and Henry's wife was a scarecrow. Off they went to get their wives for the next dance.

Maggie didn't even see Mrs. Murphy. She must be in the crowd somewhere. The band was playing a slow song now and everyone was hitting the dance floor. What a great evening it was turning out to be. A bunny, announcing herself, came over to talk to Maggie. It was Jane from Lockmore Jewellers. Maggie told her how nice it was that she donated a prize for the best costume.

"It's going to be hard to judge," she said. "Some costumes were bought or rented while others made their costume. Some of the ideas were quite amazing. Like the person who made twelve stuffed asparagus, then wrapped them around their body and came as a bunch of asparagus."

"Who was that?" asked Maggie.

"The girl that works for you, Julie, and her husband is a bunch of grapes. Great imagination and great sewing skills too."

"She is good at a lot of things, that's for sure."

"Well, I would say so far that both of them are a contender," said Jane.

"Have you seen Mrs. Murphy's costume yet?" Maggie asked.

"No, not yet why?"

"Well, she is wearing a cowgirl outfit, homemade as well and tied to each arm is a slice of toast. She calls herself a toasted western."

"Oh my, really, that's hilarious; I'll have to check her out. Talk to you later Maggie."

Maggie carried on filling glasses with punch. Ray had come by earlier with bags and bags of chips, pretzels and cheese snacks. Maggie kept refilling the bowls when they got low. People had incredible appetites after coming off the dance floor.

CHAPTER 11

"Hi, Maggie!" yelled the Queen of Hearts. "It's me, Kim."

Kim rushed over to the punch table to show Maggie her costume. Maggie gave her a big hug.

"You look so cute, Kim. Nice costume. I'm glad you could make it."

"Thanks, Maggie, you look beautiful in your barmaid costume. I'm glad you still wear it. Everyone knows where to find you and well, it suits you. I think it has become a tradition."

"You're sweet, where is your other half?" said Maggie.

"My rugged football player is over there talking to the construction worker. I can only imagine what the conversation must be," laughed Kim.

"Yes, that would be interesting," said Maggie. "I'm just so happy at the great time everyone seems to be having. It is such a perfect night for it too. People are even strolling around the grounds, absorbing all that nature has to offer."

As Maggie was talking to Kim, she could see a doctor coming her way. He was dressed in surgical scrubs, a surgeon's cap, a mask and a stethoscope around his neck. She also noticed he was tall, with a nice build and blonde hair. He came right up beside her and introduced himself to her and Kim. It was one of Maggie's customers, Stew. With some of the costumes Maggie didn't know if the people were actually what they were wearing. Was the construction worker actually in construction and was Stew actually a doctor?

"Are you really a doctor?" asked Maggie. "I know you work in Hainesley, but I thought you were a teacher."

"You're right, Maggie, I borrowed everything from my brother. I thought this was more interesting than coming as a schoolteacher with a mask on."

"Well, you look great," said Maggie.

"Thank you, Maggie and so do you. I thought it would be nice if I took you away from the punch table and had a dance with you, maybe Kim could watch the table. You deserve to have at least one dance."

"That's very nice of you, but ..." she said, as she was looking at Kim.

"Now you two go and enjoy your dance or even two," Kim said, looking at Maggie. "I'll be right here watching the punch table."

There was nothing more Maggie could say as Stew took her hand and led her to the dance floor. A slow dance was up first, and Stew was a very good dancer. They chatted throughout the dance. Stew lived in Hainesley. He came to Carleton Falls once in a while to visit his sister who moved here a couple of years ago. That's when he would come into the bakery. The music changed tempo now and all of the people on the dance floor were swinging their arms and moving their feet. Everyone was having such a great time. Maggie was finally enjoying herself too, thanks to Stew. It certainly was a sight to see, two vegetables, a strawberry, a hotdog, a couple of pumpkins, a robot, a nurse, a sailor, a house plant, a policeman and a whole lot more dancing up a storm. The music changed its tempo again. Stew looked at Maggie and asked her for one more. She nodded her head in approval. They were both quiet this time enjoying each other's company. Maggie was just watching the crowd and thinking Mrs. Murphy may need help shortly with the food.

As she looked to see if Kim was still at the punch table her eyes glanced at the front door. Standing in the doorway was a man dressed in a Lone Ranger costume. He was tall with dark hair. A very robust man and he wore the costume like he was actually playing the part. Another great costume Maggie thought. But who was he? She watched as he went over to the punch table. The ranger and the Queen of Hearts were in deep conversation. But then Kim was a very outgoing person and could talk to anybody. She handed him a glass of punch and he went to talk to a group of people standing near the doorway. The music stopped and the band was going to take a break.

"Thank you for the dances, Stew," Maggie said. "I really enjoyed it."

"I did as well, Maggie. I'll walk you back to the punch table."

"How was the dancing, you two," said Kim, as Maggie and Stew approached.

"It was fun," said Maggie. "Stew is a great dancer. Thanks for watching the table, Kim."

"If you need a break later, let me know," said Kim.

As Kim left, Maggie said goodbye to Stew. During their dance Stew had mentioned he was waiting for some friends to arrive. He was having a great time as everyone seemed to be having. She noticed Mrs. Murphy and the ladies' auxiliary opening the back doors of the barn, getting ready to bring in the food. Maggie went to help them. They had a ramp from the truck and rolled the steamers down the ramp and into the barn. The food was nice and warm, ready to be served cafeteria style. Everyone lined up with a plate in hand. They only had to ask for what they wanted, and the ladies served them. The ribs and sauerkraut were a hit just like last year, as well as the red potato salad. The homemade pierogies and cabbage rolls were a close second. Even the sausage done in celery, onions and mushrooms was a contender too. Needless to say, the ladies out did themselves and the food was exceptional. With only a couple of people left to serve, the ladies decided to help themselves. Maggie helped herself to the cabbage rolls and the red potato salad. The food was delicious as always, she thought.

She quickly ate so she could get her desserts on the tables. While the ladies were still cleaning up, Maggie used the carts to bring some of the desserts from the truck. She arranged them on the tables nicely and began to slice the cakes, pies and strudel. This time the desserts were put on small plates. The people could come and help themselves. Maggie could add more as the desserts ran out. The boxed cookies and pumpkin tarts were also put out for people to help themselves. The band was getting ready to start the dancing. They announced that the desserts were ready and for the people to go and help themselves. Maggie's desserts were flying off the tables. A man dressed as a deck of cards told Maggie her cheesecake was the best he ever had. He said it was high end restaurant worthy. So much so that he wanted to order some and pick them up every Monday. She was really making a name for herself.

The music was in high gear again and the people were dancing their hearts out. Maggie enjoyed watching the people having a good time. There wasn't much to clean up, just a few pieces of strudel left. The punch bowl was getting a little low and could use a refill. Maggie reached under the table to get a bottle of fruit juice. She opened it and added it to the punch bowl. One more she thought and added it as well. Now for the soda pop, then she added the limes, lemons and oranges. The last thing was the ice. It was time to relax, she thought and have a glass of punch herself. But first she wanted to put the carts away at the back of the barn. Ted was nice enough to let them use them.

Mrs. Murphy was enjoying herself with the other ladies. They were all on the dance floor dancing as if they had been waiting for this all year. Maggie finally got herself a glass of punch and backed a few feet away from the table, standing there watching the crowd with her glass of punch in her hand and her foot tapping the floor, taking it all in. Her eyes came upon the man in the Lone Ranger costume that she'd seen earlier. He was approaching in her direction. She couldn't take her eyes off of him. She was intrigued at his physique and how well the costume fit, in all the right places. His arms were very muscular and his waist trim. His hat completed his full persona. Who was this masked ranger? she wondered. He must be coming for some punch, she thought. As she went to offer him some, Maggie tripped, and her punch flew across the table and into his face.

"I needed that, thanks, I was a little thirsty."

"Oh my, I'm so sorry, I tripped," said Maggie, so embarrassed, and handed him a towel.

The ranger took off his hat and mask so he could wipe his face.

"Jack, it's you!" Maggie said loudly, taking off her mask.

"Maggie," he said, "it's you, and now I know why it happened, you're accident-prone. You're out to get me," he chuckled.

"Jack, I didn't even know it was you, I'm sorry," she said.

"I forgive you, again," Jack laughed. "We have to stop meeting like this. Do you have any water, the punch is quite sticky?"

"Yes, Jack, here you go."

"Would you mind pouring some in my hands?"

Maggie poured some water into Jack's hands and watched Jack as he splashed the water on his face, and towel dried it. The gaze from his hazel eyes were just as warm and gentle, as she remembered.

"That's much better," he said, as he brushed his hand through his hair. "At least the hat saved the hair from being sticky."

"Again, Jack, I'm so sorry."

"It could have happened to anyone, let's just forget about it. If I had known it was you, I would have come to see you and say hello," said Jack.

"The masks have made it an interesting evening, that's for sure," said Maggie. "All the different costumes are amazing. Your costume is great too, Jack. You look so good in it. What made you think of a Lone Ranger's costume, quite unique?"

"Well, he wore a mask and was a ranger, so I thought since I'm a park ranger, why not and I am from Texas. I'm a park ranger at the Carleton Falls State Park, Maggie. I actually take care of it. It's my job to look after the people that come to stay there."

"I didn't know Jack, why haven't I seen you there before? It wasn't my first camping trip ... but it was the first one this year, so, I should know better than anyone that things change, sometimes too quickly," said Maggie feeling a little remorse.

"That's okay, Maggie, I guess I should have introduced myself. I'm Jack Kincaid, nice to meet you and you are?"

"I'm Maggie Sinclaire, Jack, nice to meet you."

"Now that we have formally introduced ourselves, what do you say about having this dance, Maggie?"

"Thank you, Jack, I would love to."

Jack asked the cat nearby if she would mind watching the punch table. She told Jack she would be glad to. Jack and Maggie walked to the dance floor. The band was playing a slow song. As Maggie stood in front of Jack, he placed one hand on her waist and took her one hand in his. Maggie placed her other hand on his shoulder. Jack was quite a bit taller than Maggie. He had to be over six feet tall, she thought, as her head didn't quite make it to his shoulders. His slow dancing was perfect, as he led her around the floor. His physical stature was that of a park ranger. Everything about him called out park ranger, why didn't I see that? she thought. The embarrassment she felt every time they met had clouded her judgment.

"Jack," she said, "I want to apologize for the negative attitude I gave you at the camp. I should have known you were just trying to help me, and I was too proud to let you, I'm sorry."

"It's okay Maggie, at least I got a great cup of coffee out of it," he chuckled. "But honestly, I did enjoy your company."

"Thanks, Jack, for understanding."

CHAPTER 12

As Jack and Maggie danced, Maggie placed her head on Jack's chest. Jack drew Maggie in a little closer, making her feel secure, their bodies like one, as he guided her around the floor. As Jack put his chin beside Maggie's head, he could smell the scent of her hair. It smelled like fresh berries and wildflowers on a spring day. Her body felt good next to his, something he hadn't felt in a while. She looked a little different with her hair up, a little less outdoorsy, he thought, but still just as beautiful.

Jack and Maggie barely took a break from dancing as the night went on. He was just as good at fast dancing as he was at slow. But Maggie preferred the slow, feeling Jack's arm around her. She hadn't felt that sense of security in a long time. Jack felt like home. The rest of the people couldn't help but notice the amount of time they were spending on the dance floor. The people looked on as the barmaid and the ranger danced around the room.

The song had ended, and one band member said that the winner of the costume contest would be announced shortly. Everyone stopped talking to hear the announcement, now impatiently waiting. Who was it going to be? The band member came back to the microphone.

"Ladies and gentlemen, our three judges, Jane Lockmore, Ted Mason and Ray Fletcher have agreed on one winner. They wanted me to express that it was a very difficult decision as everyone had outstanding costumes. Those that get an honorary mention are: a bunch of grapes, the marshmallow, the mermaid and, finally, the toasted western. Because of the great turnout we had and the wonderful costumes, Ray Fletcher has gifted from city hall to these people, a dinner for two at the Parker Alexander Fine Dining Restaurant in Hainesley. Congratulations! Now, what everyone has been waiting for. This costume was original, homemade and very well done. The winner of the prize from Lockmore Jewellers is . . . a bunch of asparagus."

The crowd was clapping and cheering. Julie, who was wearing the costume went on stage and thanked the judges and Lockmore Jewellers. Her prize was wrapped in beautiful gold and silver shiny paper, with a large black and white bow. Julie pulled the bow off and ripped the paper revealing a dark purple box. She opened the lid and inside was a gold locket with chain and matching earrings. The locket was shaped like a heart with small diamonds all around the outside and an emerald shaped heart in the center. Just stunning, she thought. She was so happy, and people went over to congratulate her. Maggie and Jack went over as well.

"Congrats Julie, you deserve it. You did a really nice job sewing your costume," Maggie said as she turned to introduce Jack. "Jack, this is Julie and Julie, this is Jack."

"Nice to meet you, Jack," said Julie.

"Likewise," said Jack. "That is one great costume."

"Thank you both, now I need to fine my bunch of grapes," she laughed.

Julie went off to find Will and Jack and Maggie headed back to the punch table. The crowd had thinned out as people had left after the winner was announced. Mrs. Murphy saw Maggie talking to Jack and went over to introduce herself. It was nice to see Maggie with a man, she thought. The poor girl was always busy working. Jack and Mrs. Murphy seemed to hit it off. Jack was very charismatic, and Mrs. Murphy was soaking it all up. They could have talked all night, but Jack had asked Mrs. Murphy if she would watch the punch table for Maggie, as the cat had left. He wanted to take Maggie for a stroll before the night ended. Mrs. Murphy agreed.

The night air was crisp and cool as they walked past the stacked bales of hay and the candle-lit pumpkins. The string of lights that Maggie and Mrs. Murphy had put up gave a nice, enchanting glow, along with the shimmering moonlight. Jack took off his jacket and put it around Maggie's shoulders. The warmth from his body clung to his jacket, embracing her, as the lingering heat left her wanting more. Under his jacket he was dressed in a nice dress shirt and tie. His broad shoulders fit the shirt nicely and he was definitely the right build to be wearing a Texas Ranger costume, thought

Maggie. She then asked him how he made out the morning it rained. Did all the campsites get flooded and did everyone have to leave? she wanted to know. Jack explained the camps that were on a slope were wet but okay. The rest of the campsites were flooded, so the ones using tents came and stayed at the community center cabin that was built in the spring especially for times like that.

"We want the campers to be safe at all times. It sure was a hectic day. But we managed. I went to check on you, but you were gone. Did you leave the night before?"

"No, I left that morning very early. I got drenched but that was about it. Jasper and I made it home okay. It just took us a little longer because traffic was slow. I was thinking of you, hoping you were all right. But I didn't know much about you. I thought you were just camping like me."

"It's nice to know you were interested," said Jack. "I was actually camping like you as I had taken some vacation days. That's why I was out of uniform. I never even thought about telling you, every camper gets an envelope given to them when they rent a spot. I guess I just figured you knew who I was because of the brochure inside with my picture on it."

"That would explain things. I told them that I had been there before, and didn't need one. They probably thought it was in the summer. Again, my fault."

"How's your dog, Jasper?" asked Jack.

"He's good, staying with a friend of mine tonight."

"I'm glad he's good, Maggie. He's a very nice dog."

"Thanks, Jack, I think so too. Since you work at the park you must know Kim and Dale, they run the little store."

"Yes," said Jack, as he sat down next to Maggie sitting on a bale of hay. "I have met them on a few occasions. They're very nice people but I don't get over to see them very often. The visitors are my first priority."

"Kim and her husband are good friends of mine. Kim and I met during our grade school years when our parents sent us to the same summer camp. My father even back then wanted me to learn about the great outdoors. Kim used to cry the whole time she was there wanting to go home. I asked her one day if she wanted to be my friend and we have remained friends all these years. Once in a while when my dad and I went camping, my dad would ask if Kim wanted to come. It's funny how she is working in a store in a State Park now. She loves the outdoors as much as I do."

"It's nice you both have remained friends. That's very special," said Jack.

"Where did you grow up?" asked Maggie.

"I was born in Texas but at an early age we moved to a small town called Wainsboro in Canada. My father was offered a job at a provincial park as a park warden; here he would be called a park ranger. His job was to patrol the area and make sure the visitors were safe. He loved it there and we always went camping. My mom loved camping too. We would go fishing, canoeing, and have campfires and star gaze. I have a lot of good memories; it was a family thing, the three of us together. I always felt at one with nature, it's a great feeling. I went to school to become a park ranger like my dad, and I worked there as well. Then my dad passed away and my mom went to live with her sister. So, I decided to go back to Texas and here I am a park ranger at Carleton Falls State Park."

"Sorry about your dad, Jack. I'm glad you decided to come here and live out your dreams."

"Thanks, Maggie, I appreciate that," said Jack. "I think maybe we should go back in now."

"Yes, Mrs. Murphy will think we got lost."

The dance was coming to a close. Jack helped Maggie and Mrs. Murphy with the tables. The band was packing up their electronics. Only a few people from the church remained, helping to empty the garbage and recycling containers. The guests were asked to put paper plates, plastic utensils and plastic glasses into recycling containers, so they were kept separate from the garbage. Maggie would drop by tomorrow and take down the lights. It was too dark to do that now, especially the ones outside. She would also sweep the barn and put the wagon wheels and butter churns back where they were. She was going to ask Jack to move the bales of hay to one section of the barn, so Ted Mason wouldn't have to do it. Mrs. Murphy went outside to collect some pumpkins and some corn stalks for the children's Halloween Party at the church. Mr. Mason had said to help ourselves. They would make great decorations and maybe some of the children could carve some pumpkins as well. With Mrs. Murphy's car loaded, she said her goodbyes to Maggie and Jack. The people from church had also left. Maggie and Jack were just waiting for the last band member. He finally loaded his car, and he was off. Maggie and Jack turned off the lights and closed the barn doors.

"It's almost midnight, would you like to get a coffee," asked Maggie.

"Sure, I could use one, do you know of a place?"

"As a matter of fact, I do. The best coffee in town, follow me," said Maggie.

They got into their cars and Maggie took the lead. It didn't take long to get to Magpie. She pulled into the parking lot with Jack right behind her. Jack was impressed with her bakery. It was a great location and could see her doing well. Maggie took Jack in the back door. Once inside she started to make coffee.

"It will only take a few minutes Jack. Would you like something to eat with the coffee?"

"Sure, Maggie, what do you suggest?"

"Well, you look like a shortbread or a scone person."

"Yes please," said Jack.

"Well, which one, Jack."

"Both would be nice, Maggie. Would you have some butter and honey for the scones? My Grams always used butter and honey."

"Of course, Jack, I remember. Butter and honey it is."

Jack watched Maggie as she dressed a plate with a few pieces of shortbread and a couple of scones. Very particular, he thought, as she arranged them on the plate. She definitely had a way of doing things. She placed the plate in front of Jack and went to get two cups for the coffee. She took two mugs from a shelf above the sink and filled them. Lastly, she put butter and honey on the table.

"I warmed the scones up just a little so the butter and honey would melt into the pastry. I hope you enjoy it, Jack."

"This looks great, Maggie, and the coffee smells just like it did at the campsite. My Grams would have liked you, Maggie Sinclaire."

Jack started on the warm scones first. The butter and honey melted into all the nooks and crannies and sank to the bottom layer of the scone. Jack couldn't wait any longer to take a bite. The combination of butter, honey and scone was amazing and the look on Jack's face was pure pleasure and satisfaction. Maggie looked on and smiled.

"Will you join me, Maggie?"

"Not tonight, Jack, just coffee for me."

"Well, I guess you know what you're missing, because the scones and shortbread are delicious."

The rest of the night they were in full conversation. Jack really liked her bakery and the idea of having a drive-thru. He thought Maggie was a very smart businesswoman and an excellent baker as well. It was late and Maggie still had to pick up Jasper if Charlie was still up. It wouldn't be the first time Jasper stayed all night with Charlie but if she could, she would rather take him home. Jack told Maggie now that he knew where she was most of the time; he would come and visit her at the bakery.

CHAPTER 13

"Thanks Charlie, I didn't want to wake you last night," said Maggie as Jasper tried to bypass Charlie to get to her. "Hey Jasper, I missed you, boy."

"That's okay Maggie; we were just fine, like I said, anytime."

"Thanks, Charlie . . . bye."

Jasper couldn't wait to get into the passenger seat of the car. He knew he was going to see Flora and Tilly. Finally ready to go, they were headed to Magpie. The girls had already opened the bakery. Cars were pulling in and out, very busy for early in the morning, she thought. They usually got busy after church. But busy anytime was good. Maggie's main goal today was to make the cheesecakes that the deck of cards ordered for Monday. She would have to come in every Sunday to make sure his order would be ready. It's not very often that Mr. Parker Alexander from Fine Dining wanted to order cheesecakes from an unknown bakery. This was very special and hopefully the word would get around.

Maggie whipped all of the ingredients for the cheesecakes, then she filled her nonstick springform pans containing a cookie crumble on the bottom. The springform pan would make it easy to remove the cakes later. Into the oven they went. Maggie always used her baked cheesecake recipe for her round cheesecakes. She found that her baked recipe gave her cakes a richer flavour and a creamier texture instead of her no-bake recipe. This is probably why Mr. Alexander thought they were restaurant worthy. Her no-bake recipe she would use for cheesecake squares.

Julie went out front to help Liz and Ella. Church was over and the bakery was even busier than before. Mrs. Murphy was out front and wanted to see her pendant, from last night. Julie couldn't help but show it off and rightfully so; it was beautiful.

"Hey there, my lady, how's it going?" Kim said, as she peeked through the back doorway, watching Maggie cleaning the counter.

"Hi, Kim. I thought you had gone back to the park last night."

"No, Dale wanted to stay the night after the dance, so we booked a stay-over at Katie's. We're just heading back now. Dale's having a coffee, and I wanted to see you before we headed back. Do you have time for a break?"

"Sure, good timing let's head out back," said Maggie.

"So, what's going on with you and Jack? I didn't even know you too had met."

"Well Kim, do you remember when I mentioned about a man that was annoying me and being arrogant. It was the day you gave me a coffee because I was upset?"

"Yes, and that man was Jack?" asked Kim.

"Yes, but I didn't know he was the park ranger. He was trying to help me when I fell into the river and again when I was in the rowboat. I was embarrassed and didn't think I needed any help. We talked about it last night and he just laughed about it."

"Great, Maggie, you seem to really like Jack."

"Now don't go putting two and two together, Kim. We are just two adults being friendly to each other and enjoying each other's company. He's gone back to the park. You will probably see him more than me."

"You two had such a connection at the dance. Everyone was talking about how good the two of you looked together and how well you danced together," stated Kim. "Look at this."

"You took a picture of us together?"

"Yep, to show you how well the barmaid and the Texas Ranger go together," said Kim, showing the picture from her phone.

"It is a good picture, Kim. But we are just friends. If anything changes you will be the first to know," laughed Maggie. "I'm too busy to even consider it."

"Okay, I just want you to meet someone nice to share your life with, like me and Dale."

"Thanks, Kim, maybe someday."

Just then a car drove up to the back of the bakery; it was Dale waiting for Kim.

"Looks like my guy is ready to go home," said Kim. "Love ya hun and remember I'm just a phone call away."

"I know, love you too, have a safe drive and give Dale a hug."

Maggie stood waving as the car pulled out, thinking about the friends she has had in her life. They were all really family. She was fortunate to have caring people around her. Maggie went inside to take her cheesecakes from the oven. Julie was a step ahead of her. They were already in the cooler and boxed waiting for Mr. Alexander to pick them up tomorrow morning.

"Thanks, Julie, you're the best."

"Right back at you, boss."

Maggie nodded and smiled. "I think I will pick up Jasper at Flora's and head out. I have to stop at Mr. Mason's barn and take down the lights and clean up. You try and leave early if you can Julie, enjoy the rest of your day. Liz and Ella can close up. By the way, your pendent is gorgeous. You so deserved it," Maggie said, seeing a sudden big smile on Julie's face and a nod of appreciation.

As the days passed it was business as usual. The children's Halloween party had come and gone with Maggie's cookies and cupcakes a success as usual. Mr. Alexander was so happy with his cheesecakes; he ordered a few more for his other restaurant. Business was good and with the weather getting colder, more coffee was being sold. Winter seemed to be moving closer, but fall wasn't giving in just yet. Maggie had expected Jack to come for a visit since it was the middle of November. She wondered if he was just being polite at the dance and never intended to stop in to see her.

Mr. Sands had stopped by to let Maggie know they would be starting the drive-thru any day now.

She was so excited that Mrs. Murphy's idea was becoming a reality. When it was finished Maggie wanted Mrs. Murphy to be the first person through it for a free cup of coffee. Today for Maggie, however, was a busy day, preparing for Katie's luncheon tomorrow. Katie had decided on fancy bread for the people, and she would make the fillings for the sandwiches.

Maggie made six batches of bread dough. In four of the batches mixed, while kneading the dough, she added food colouring, giving each of the four batches a different colour and the other two staying the same. Each batch of dough was set aside to rise. After the dough had risen, she then divided each batch into four smaller batches. Taking one small batch from each, she then rolled out one piece of coloured dough, then another and another and finally one more. These four different coloured rolled out pieces of dough were layered on top of each other, brushing a little water on each, better to adhere the layers. Then she rolled up the dough into a log and placed it into a bread pan. She also did alternate layers of dough with no food colouring. Maggie would alternate one layer of regular coloured dough with one layer of food colouring dough and so on, brushing a little water in-between each layer as before. Having the four layers in place, she rolled it up into a log and placed it into a bread pan as well. Maggie would repeat the process until all the dough was rolled up and put into bread pans. Again, the dough had to rest before they went into the oven. Once cooked and cooled

Maggie would cut the crust from the bread, then slice the bread and put it into bags to stay fresh. All Katie had to do was make sandwiches using her fillings and slice them into fours diagonally. The crust was turned into breadcrumbs and also sold at the bakery.

In-between the rest times for the bread Maggie would be working on the Yule logs. The batter was mixed and ready to go into six pans. Maggie used her largest jelly roll pans. Once they were cooked, she would cut the cake horizontally across the pan from side to side, which would give her two large cakes. Then she would roll them up to give her two large Yule logs. Then she would cut them both into thirds, giving her six small Yule logs per pan. It would work out perfectly with one to spare. It didn't take Maggie too long and into the oven they went.

Maggie was thinking of Jasper at Flora's wondering if he was tired and sleeping most of the day. Maggie took him to the dog park yesterday after work. He hadn't seen Mandy this time but met a collie named Nova. They got along really well, but not as well as Jasper and Mandy did. Maybe it was because Mandy was a smaller dog than Nova. Maggie enjoyed talking to his owner. She works in the advertising business and was telling Maggie about the companies that now use her business. It had taken a while for her name to get around but now she is doing quite well. The lady was impressed with Maggie's bakery and told her if she was ever in need of baked goods, she would give Maggie a call and Maggie said the same to her. They exchanged business cards as well, because you just never know when they might be needed.

The bread had completed their final rise and were ready for the oven. The Yule log cakes were done and ready to come out of the oven. She let the cakes cool just a bit as she wanted to roll them while they were still slightly warm. Each large cake in the pan was divided to make two cakes. Maggie carefully took one at a time and placed it on the non-stick roll cake roller. Carefully, she rolled up the cake, then unrolled the cake and then took out the roller. She rolled it up again by hand and cut the large roll into three even rolls. This was the time-consuming part of the bake but necessary. Once she had her small Yule logs and they were completely cooled, she set each on a piece of cake board and put them into plastic bags to keep fresh for Katie's luncheon, tomorrow. Maggie repeated the process until she had 36 Yule logs packaged and put into the walk-in. During the packaging of the Yule logs all the fancy bread was taken out of the oven and left to cool.

Julie had finished her orders early and made the chocolate slab cake for Maggie. It wasn't a part of Katie's plan, but Maggie wanted to make a dessert for the luncheon to surprise Katie. Julie called her last week to let her know not to make anything, with the baby coming Katie had enough to do. With the slab cake finished and boxed Julie helped Maggie by taking the crust off of the fancy bread, slicing each loaf then bagging them. Julie even made enough chocolate icing for Maggie to take with her tomorrow, so the people could spread it over their Yule logs. Julie was always there to back Maggie up when the workload was heavy. They were definitely a good team.

Now all Maggie had to do was the cream filling for inside the Yule log, then pack as much as she could tonight, including decorations and the cake ingredients she would need to show them how to make one. The girls closed up the bakery with Maggie having a few more things to do. Finally finished she poured a couple of coffees. She decided to take some Jasper cookies with her and a coffee for Flora. Jasper loved his cookies and now it was time to see if Tilly liked them too. Just something else she should be selling, but there were only so many hours in a day.

CHAPTER 14

Maggie and Jasper had a good night's sleep. So good in fact, they didn't even hear the alarm until someone knocking at the front door woke Maggie up. She turned off her alarm clock, put on her slippers and robe and headed to the front door. Who could that be? I don't usually have people come over to see me at the house, she thought. Maggie opened the door and saw Mrs. Abigail standing there with a worried look on her face.

"Hi, Mrs. Abigail, is everything all right?"

"No dear, not really. I took Fluffy out for some fresh air, and she went under your porch. I took my eyes off her for just a minute, and she hopped over here and under a board she went. I tried to coax her out with a carrot, but she wouldn't come out. I was wondering if Jasper could get her to come out."

"Don't worry Mrs. Abigail. We will get her. Jasper, here boy," Maggie called.

Jasper came running to the front door, wagging his tail. Maggie went out on the porch with Mrs. Abigail and told Jasper to find Fluffy. Jasper knew Fluffy because he would play with the bunny and Mrs. Abigail's cat Mittens whenever he would go over to her house. Jasper was jumping and barking letting Fluffy know to come out and play. It only took a few minutes and sure enough she came right out and over to Jasper to play. Maggie and Mrs. Abigail smiled at each other.

"Oh, thank you, Jasper," said Mrs. Abigail as she picked up Fluffy. "Thank you too, Maggie. I was lucky you were home."

"You're welcome, Mrs. Abigail, we'll have to get together for a play day. Jasper would like that."

"Okay dear, anytime, just call me," said Mrs. Abigail as she carried Fluffy home.

Back inside Maggie looked at the clock, oh my, she thought running late again. She turned on the coffee maker, gave Jasper some kibble and in the shower she went. Hmm . . . what to take to the bakery to change into? she thought. Should she look professional and dress up? She was a jeans and sweatshirt type of gal. Maybe today a little of both, black jeans and a fancy shirt. After all, she will be wearing an apron most of the time.

With a coffee in hand and Jasper at her side, they were off to the bakery and Flora's. After dropping Jasper off she would have two hours to get Katie's order packed up and off to the bed and breakfast for set up. From the roadway she noticed a truck called Sands 'n Sons Construction. As she pulled in around the back of the bakery, she saw Mr. Sands talking to some of his workers. She couldn't believe it; it was about to happen. The drive-thru was coming to life.

"Good morning, Mr. Sands, nice to see you."

"Well, Miss Sinclaire, today's the day. We will try our best not to disturb your customers. My men will be putting up signs and using pylons to keep traffic away from the area being worked on. Other than that, business should be like any other day.

"Thank you, Mr. Sands, I will be gone part of the day. Should you need anything, just ask Julie inside or if you need me just call my cell, here's my card. This is so exciting."

"You have yourself a good day, Miss Sinclaire."

"You too, Mr. Sands," said Maggie as she smiled and walked toward the car to let Jasper out.

"C'mon boy, let's go see Tilly."

After going through the back door and changing in the back room, Maggie came into the baking area.

"Good morning, Julie, I'm just going to pack up and head to the bed and breakfast. I told Mr. Sands if he needs anything, to ask you. I have my cell, if you need to call me."

"I'm sure everything will be fine. I'm so happy for you, I mean us, and this drive-thru is going to be great."

"Yes, I think so too," said Maggie still smiling. "Now it's time to get the car packed. I want this to go smoothly for Katie. If I get there early enough, I can make the sandwiches for her."

Maggie grabbed the boxes of fancy bread and took them to the car. Next were the Yule logs all nicely packed in a box as well. Into the walk-in she went to get the Yule log filling and icing. Inside the box she placed all the decorations as well. One more trip to the car and that should be it, she thought. Nope, Julie reminded her about the slab cake she had made for the luncheon. With the car full, Maggie decided to go back in to double check. All the dry ingredients were still sitting on the counter. I can't forget those, or I won't be able to show the ladies how to make the logs, Maggie thought. She needed to take a deep breath and focus on what she needed to take. The start of the drive-thru was overwhelming her. It was a good thing she would be gone for most of the afternoon.

"Well, I have everything I need, Julie. Have a good day. I will see you later," said Maggie.

Maggie was off to the bed and breakfast. The weather still wasn't very cold considering it was the middle of November. Soon it would be Thanksgiving, a lot of customers will be phoning in their orders. I must remember to have Julie put out the last date for orders sign, she thought. I better call her now.

"Hi, Julie, I just wanted to remind you about the date sign for orders."

"It's been out for two days now, it's all good Maggie."

"What's going on, everything all right, Julie?" asked Maggie as she heard something break.

"Yes," Julie laughed, "one of the workers cut a hole in the building for the drive-thru window and leaned in to order a coffee. Anna was a little surprised and dropped a coffee mug. We better put that on our list of supplies to get."

"Poor Anna. Okay, Julie, see you later."

Maggie pulled into the parking lot. Not a space to be had. Even the overflow parking lot was being used. I hope there aren't more than thirty-five people for the luncheon, she thought. Probably people renting the rooms as well. She parked along the side door and opened the hatchback. In she carried a couple of boxes to the kitchen. Tony met her on the way and went out to her car and retrieved the rest.

"Where should I park, Tony? Most of the spots are taken."

"You're fine right where you are, Maggie. We're not expecting any deliveries today."

"Thanks, Tony, where is Katie?"

"She was told by the doctor yesterday afternoon to get some bed rest and stay off her feet for a week or two. She has just been doing a little too much lately."

"Why didn't she tell me, I could have come over to help her weeks ago?"

"Well, we both know how stubborn Katie is. She has to do everything herself."

"Yes, I know what that's like. So, I suppose I'm on my own with the luncheon?"

"Well, you have me, if needed," said Tony.

"You need a break too, but then you're not the pregnant one either," she said, with a hint of laughter. "I think you have more than enough to keep you busy. So, where are the people for the luncheon?"

"Our guests are in the common room getting acquainted with each other waiting for Nancy to bring them to you here in the kitchen. Probably in forty-five minutes."

"Perfect, that will give me time to make the fancy sandwiches and get the tables ready with each person's Yule log. Did Katie make the fillings, do you know?"

"I don't know Maggie. Check the fridge, if not help yourself to whatever you need. Thanks, Maggie."

"You're welcome and you can tell Katie not to worry. I will do my best."

Tony left the kitchen to carry on with his chores and run the bed and breakfast. Maggie put the coffee on first. She wanted to make sure it would be ready and didn't want to forget about it. She then put her Yule log filling and icing into the fridge, then looked through the fridge and found three bowls labeled luncheon. Katie was pretty particular when it came to food and labeling it. She would put the date when made on it and she always kept her kitchen immaculate. This was perfect Maggie thought as she opened the bags of bread. Having washed her hands, she put the slices on the counter in rows. She was going to do this like an assembly line. The first filling was tuna salad. She spooned a large dollop on half of the slices on the table. Then she took the other slices and put them on top of the tuna slices. She took a long cutting knife from the knife block and cut each sandwich diagonally into halves then again into quarters. Maggie then placed the sandwiches on a fancy plate and into the fridge. She repeated the same procedure, using a different filling. This time Katie had made a crab filling. Another great choice, Maggie thought. Katie was known for adding some onion, green pepper and a little pickle cut up fine, to her crab salad. Having finished the crab sandwiches, Maggie opened the lid of the third bowl. Egg salad, it smelled wonderful and Maggie's favourite.

As she laid out the slices of bread, and spooned the egg salad onto the bread she couldn't help but think about Carleton Falls State Park. She was thinking of the egg salad sandwich she was eating in the rowboat and that led her to thinking about her line getting stuck and falling backwards into the boat. Then she thought of Jack trying to help her. Why wasn't he coming to see her? Was there something between the two of them like Kim said? He must be quite busy, she thought instead.

"How's it going, Maggie? Tony sent me to see if I can help you."

"Hi, Nancy," she said awakened from her thoughts. "If you could put thirty-five placemats on the tables and space them out a bit with a napkin and a knife on each placemat, that would be great."

Maggie finished all the sandwiches with the fillings and bread she had left. Nancy had pushed all the doors back into the wall. This dining room was adjoined to the kitchen with sliding doors separating the two rooms. It was very convenient and was also used as an overflow for extra dining with a different menu, as well. They had a larger more formal dining room used for supper, for the people that stayed with them. The smaller one if not being used could be set up for those wanting breakfast in the morning.

Maggie was going to do her demonstration on the kitchen island. Here she put her dry ingredients, a bowl, a jelly roll pan and a wooden spoon. She brought the coffee and warming plate plus takeout cups to the island as well. The last thing was to put a Yule log on each placemat.

"Thank you, Nancy, for helping. You can let the people in now," said Maggie ready to begin.

Nancy led the people in through the dining room doors that are across the hall from the common room. The majority of people coming in were ladies but there were three men as well. They looked like an eager bunch and very friendly. People just out to enjoy themselves. There weren't many, if any, demonstrations on how to do anything, in Carleton Falls. Maybe Katie was on to something. It didn't even have to be baking it could be any demonstration. It could be sewing, cooking recipes, painting, crafts and many other things. Something for her to think about after the baby was born.

CHAPTER 15

Maggie watched the people as they piled in.

"Please take a spot, any spot where there is a Yule log on a placemat. When everyone is seated, we will begin."

Everyone had a seat and was waiting instructions from Maggie.

"Hello and welcome to our first Yule log making demonstration. For those of you who don't know me, my name is Maggie Sinclaire. I own Magpie Bakery here in Carleton Falls. For those I do know, I'm glad to see you here. To everyone, thank you for coming. First, I am going to show you how to make a Yule log from scratch. I see most of you have brought a pen and paper. For those who didn't I have pen and paper up here for you to use. The Yule log I'm making is the same size you have in front of you. The ovens here are not large enough to accommodate thirty-five Yule logs, which is why you have one sitting in front of you. Please leave the Yule logs as they are until later, then I will give you instructions on what to do. Please feel free to come up and watch if you wish and by all means help yourself to a cup of coffee."

As Maggie added each ingredient the group was writing it down and listening to her comments as to why she used one ingredient over another. Some of the people had questions for her as well. They even asked her if she would be doing this again. They all watched closely as Maggie put the batter into a very small jelly roll pan lined with parchment paper, then into the oven. She thought showing them this way would make it easier for them at home to remove their cake from the pan. While the cake was cooking, she told them it was time for a bite to eat and more coffee. Maggie spotted a folded table at the back of the dining room. She asked two of the men if they would mind bringing it up to the front and opening it up in front of the island. She also had them place the coffee pot and warming tray on the table along with more coffee cups. Two ladies helped her with the sandwiches, paper plates and napkins. The forks for dessert were also put on the table as well as the chocolate slab cake that Julie had made. She thanked them for helping her and announced to everyone that it was time to eat.

Maggie stood back and watched everyone talking about today's events and the Yule log recipe. They were all impressed with the fancy sandwiches and the different colours of the bread. They asked Maggie if she could do a workshop on how to make fancy bread using food colouring. Maggie told them she would talk to Katie about it. Maggie slipped away to check on the cake in the oven. It was ready, so she took it out and placed it on a wire rack to cool. The group was still enjoying their food.

She went to cut the chocolate slab cake into squares for those who were ready for dessert. What an impressive job Julie did on the cake. It was stunning and looked so inviting. The glistening chocolate icing and the glazed cherries on top looked scrumptious. Maggie got so many compliments about the cake. Do you sell these at your bakery, and do you have to order them ahead of time they asked? Maggie told them that she sells a round chocolate cake with chocolate icing everyday but a slab cake because it's quite bigger; it would have to be ordered. By now everyone was full and ready to assemble their Yule log with Maggie's instructions.

The two ladies again helped Maggie clean up and the two men folded up the table and set it against the wall. Maggie had taken out the cream filling and the icing out of the fridge and placed them on the island. She didn't want them to be too cold for spreading. Now Maggie was ready to begin. She began showing them how to remove the cake without breaking it. The cake batter had been poured onto parchment paper that she had laid over the bottom of the pan and up the sides. This being a small Yule log would be easier; a larger one would be more difficult for sure. Maggie had the proper utensils in her kitchen to aid in her baking. Things that the everyday person would not have in their kitchen. She first put a clean dish towel that had been dusted with powdered sugar on both sides over the cake. This should stop the cake from sticking to the towel. Then she showed them what they could use in their kitchen. She took a larger pan, flipped it over and put the bottom of the pan on top of the cake and towel. She then flipped over both pans, taking off the top pan revealing the parchment paper. Maggie found this better than using a wire cooling rack as sometimes the cake would crack. Carefully she took off the parchment paper to expose the cake underneath. She let the group know a cake board would work as well. She told them that that was one of the things she used at the bakery. Also, a metal or wooden pizza peel or pizza paddle with a short handle also comes in handy. With the cake on top of the towel it was ready to roll. Again, Maggie let them know that she uses a nonstick roll cake roller at her bakery but today using a towel she would show them how to roll up and unroll the cake. They all watched attentively as Maggie made a perfect roll.

"Now this is where everyone will participate with the cakes in front of them. Take your cakes out of the packaging and carefully unroll. They don't have to unroll flat just yet as the filling will do most of that," said Maggie.

Maggie walked around to each table to see if anyone needed help. There was only one person that broke their cake. It was one of the men who probably used a little too much force. Luckily Maggie had an extra one and told him not to worry. He told her that his wife was supposed to come but couldn't make it and wanted him to come in her place and make notes. She unrolled the Yule log for him and told him if he needed help going forward to let her know. She walked back up to the island and asked them to come up to the front. Maggie told them she would spoon enough filling and icing into cups for their Yule log. Once everyone was back at their table, she showed them on her Yule log how to spread the filling, telling them to go gently. Maggie was looking at the man who had broken his cake. He seemed to be doing okay on the new one, having noticed a lady beside him looking at him nodding her head. Once done she instructed them to roll it up gently with the filling inside and place the cake on the cake board provided. Now they were ready to spread the Yule log with the chocolate icing.

"Now, clean your knife off using the napkin beside you," said Maggie. "Yes, using your fingers works well too," she laughed as she saw a lady doing just that. "The ends of your Yule log will have no icing on them, just the top and sides. When you have finished icing your cake you can come up and take some decorations for your cake and then most importantly, stand back and take a look at what you've created."

Everyone was taking their time putting the chocolate on their cakes. They all wanted to do a good job. Even the man who was having trouble seemed to be enjoying this part. Now for the creativity part, people were coming up for decorations and looking at their Yule logs thinking how they wanted them to look.

"When you are done, please carefully put your cakes into these cake boxes that I'm going to pass out," said Maggie. "Just bend along the folds and your Yule log will fit nicely. If you want to keep it for Christmas, place it in the fridge to get cold, then remove it from the box, bag it and put into the freezer. Then when you want to eat it, take it out of the freezer and out of the bag and place on your counter to thaw out. I have had a great time today and you are a wonderful group of people. Thank you for your interest and I look forward to doing another one in the future."

They couldn't have been happier with their cakes. Each person before they left told Maggie they enjoyed her demonstration and would definitely come back for another one. She even got some orders for her fancy bread for the day before Thanksgiving. Maggie was surprised at how much fun she'd had as well. She really did enjoy her day, and it took her mind off of what was going on back at the bakery. Maggie collected all her things and took them out to the car. She was definitely leaving with less than she came with. Now to take out the recycling, the garbage and clean the kitchen, she thought. Then to quickly see Katie and tell her how it went.

"Hi, lady of leisure," Maggie chuckled.

"Hi, Maggie, I'm so sorry I wasn't there to help you. I wanted to be there, but my doctor gave me a warning."

"Yes, Tony told me, and we agree with your doctor too. You have been pushing yourself too much Katie. You will be quite busy once the baby is born."

"I know, you're right," said Katie. "How did it go?"

"It went great, everyone said they enjoyed it and would come again for another one. Plus, I got some orders for my fancy bread."

"That's wonderful, so maybe a few more of these demonstrating workshops next year? We'll have to plan them out better, maybe for different occasions."

"Don't get too ahead of yourself, Katie," she laughed. "We will talk about it another time. I want to get back to Magpie. Mr. Sands is constructing the drive-thru, and I can't wait to see how it looks so far. Love you and stay off your feet."

"Love you too, Maggie. Thanks again."

Maggie headed to her car, anticipating the amount of work that had been done at the bakery. Neither Julie nor Mr. Sands had called her so that was good. It didn't take her long to get back. As she approached the bakery, she drove slowly to take it all in. It was amazing the different look a drive-thru can give. She parked her car and got out to look. Mr. Sands' men had gone, and everything was tidy. The hole for the window was boarded up, maybe they will have a window tomorrow, she thought. Maggie walked through the front door seeing Liz and Ella waiting on customers. She waved as she walked by and went to see Julie to ask her about her day. She must be tired too, with all the noise and commotion going on.

"Hi, Julie, busy day?"

"Glad your back boss," Julie chuckled.

"Yeah, me too. Well, any problems?"

"Nope, everything went like clockwork. Mr. Sands' men are very considerate and professional. They don't think it will take long at all. Oh, and Ella was asked out on a date. He's one of the crew and his name is Mark. Ella is quite happy and they're going out tonight."

"That's great, Julie. I'm glad everything went well. As for Ella, I'm glad someone has noticed her. She's a great person."

"Yeah, it couldn't have been a better day around here. What about you?"

"It went even better than I could have imagined. The people were great. Some I knew others I didn't know. Everyone told me how much they enjoyed it and would come to another one. So, this might be a regular thing. Oh, and Katie couldn't help because her doctor put her on bed rest for a while."

"Oh no ... poor Katie, she's a go getter, she always needs to be busy. That must be hard for her."

"Yes, but she even looks exhausted so the rest will be good for her."

"When is she due, Maggie?"

"December seventh. So, there's not much time left and I will need to send out invitations for the baby shower soon. I think a December first baby shower should be good."

"That sounds good, Maggie. Oh, by the way, Charlie came in to see if you needed any help in the bakery. He knows you have been very busy and probably could use an extra hand," said Julie, boxing pies. "I told him I would ask you and there was always tomorrow."

"He is such a good man," said Maggie. "He is always thinking of others. The next time he comes in for something, tell him it's on the house. He's been watching Jasper for me at all hours and is always there when I need him. Maybe I will take him something tonight as well. Do we have any beef in the freezer, Julie?"

"Yep, and a bag of potatoes in the storage room."

"You're the greatest, thanks Julie. Is there any cherry pie in the walk-in?"

"I'm way ahead of you. I just boxed one and it's right here to take with you."

It didn't take long to make a Shepherd's pie for Charlie. Julie would close up the bakery so Maggie could get to Charlie's before he had his supper. Maggie also grabbed some Jasper cookies for Jasper and Tilly. She wanted to leave a treat for Tilly when she picked up Jasper. The Shepherd's pie was still quite warm, and the aroma was filling the car making Maggie and Jasper hungry. She also brought some fresh buns as well and the cherry pie. Maggie pulled up in Charlie's driveway. He must have heard the car because he was standing in his doorway.

"You didn't," he called out. "I can smell it from here. You're staying for supper, right?"

"I'd love too," said Maggie.

As Maggie entered the doorway, Jasper was there at her side.

"I have some of Jasper's kibble left Maggie, so you won't need to go home and get any for him," said Charlie.

"Perfect, Charlie, and here are some Jasper cookies for his dessert."

Charlie and Maggie enjoyed a very nice evening together. Maggie thanked him for coming by the bakery to see if she needed any help. That was very considerate of him. Maggie bringing supper and staying was a complete surprise for Charlie, and he loved every minute of it. It was nice for him to have company once in a while and if anyone could make him laugh, it was Maggie. Charlie had a down-deep-in-your soul kind of laugh which made his blue eyes sparkle. His dark hair with a hint of silver running through it and friendly smile made him very debonair. He was a very genuine, warm-hearted person and Maggie always knew she was lucky to have him in her life. They both enjoyed each other's company, but it was getting late. Maggie left her car in Charlie's driveway and with Jasper she walked across the street to their house. She couldn't wait to go to bed, Jasper beating her to it.

"Goodnight, boy."

CHAPTER 16

The bakery would be very busy today with people in and out picking up their orders for Thanksgiving. Mrs. Murphy picked up the desserts for the church community dinner they always had on Thanksgiving. Most of Carleton Falls would spend time with their families, but there were some who would be alone on holidays, like Maggie and Mrs. Murphy. There was also Jenny Smith, the shortbread lady Maggie would call her. She was a very nice lady but very lonely too. She wanted to join the choir but couldn't sing a note that anyone wanted to hear. But the choir master Randy Timms didn't have the heart to tell her she wasn't good enough. She had told him that she sings all the time at home and her bird loves it, he sings along with her. Randy didn't doubt that for a minute. Either she was tone deaf or the bird was, maybe both. Randy told her that he was happy she wanted to join and decided to put her next to a few male baritone singers in the choir. They would drown her out and her out-of-tune voice wouldn't distract the other female singers. Jenny loved singing and never missed a choir session. She was happy and even her singing was sounding better, something that Randy would say was a miracle or he was just getting used to it. Either way he was just happy his choir was still intact.

The drive-thru was coming along. Mr. Sands said they would be finished a week after Thanksgiving. Maggie had decided to put a help wanted sign up last week. She had a lot of applicants for the job. The person to be hired would primarily work at the drive-thru. A young, petite girl that was newly married came for an interview. Her name was Anna and her husband's name was Kevin. There was something about this girl that Maggie liked. If you asked her what it was, she couldn't tell you. Just something about her, she'd say. She and her husband came from Wesbridge, a city north of Hainesley. She used to work at a sandwich shop with a drive-thru, so this would be nothing new for her. Kevin had been transferred here to work at city hall. He will like working with Ray Fletcher, a nice, kindhearted man, Maggie told Anna. Anna thanked Maggie for hiring her and Maggie told her she could start in a few days.

Anna was quite happy with that as she had lots of unpacking to do and it being Thanksgiving gave her and her husband a day together.

Maggie was glad it was Thanksgiving tomorrow. The bakery would be closed, and she could use a day off. Julie invited Maggie to come to their place, but Maggie thanked her and told her she just wanted to relax and have some time to herself.

Maggie went out front to help the girls with the orders. The cakes were just flying off the shelves. The pumpkin pies were the number one seller and the pumpkin cookies she made were also a big seller. A large order for the Hainesley grocery store was picked up early in the morning. That was an order that her and Julie had stayed late to get done. She also had three people order a slab cake. They were people that came to Katie's luncheon and tried some there.

"A regular coffee to go, please," said a rugged voice.

Maggie couldn't help but look up. She thought it was Jack, but it was a trucker that stopped in for a coffee. He said he had heard of a great tasting coffee and was told to stop in if he was down this way. The word was getting out and she was glad the drive-thru was almost done. It's been a month and not a word from Jack. She talked to Kim the other day and she hasn't seen him either, but then she never really did see much of him or any park ranger as they were always too busy to drop buy the store. Mrs. Murphy and Katie were questioning her about Jack too. Even people in town have been asking her, how Jack is. I guess everyone has made their mind up about her and Jack, except Jack.

"Maggie," said Julie, your cell phone has been ringing over and over. Someone is trying to get a hold of you."

Maggie went to get her phone she had left on the counter in the back room, it was still ringing. Julie stayed out front to help Liz and Ella.

"Hello," said Maggie, "slow down Tony what's wrong? Is Katie all right? Okay I'll be right there."

Maggie went out front to tell Julie, and to let her know where she was going. Katie was on her way to the hospital and Tony wanted her to meet them there. That's all she knew. Julie told her to go and they would look after everything. Julie said she would call Flora if Maggie wasn't back when they closed.

Katie needed her and that was all she could think about. Katie was an only child, and her parents were on a trip out of the state and Tony's family didn't live close by at all. Maggie was the only person Tony could call. It didn't take her long to get to the Hainesley hospital. In she ran to the emergency. She looked in the waiting room and saw someone holding their head and blood on their face. Someone else was holding on to their arm. Others had their eyes closed waiting patiently for their turn, but Katie wasn't there. Maggie went to triage to inquire. They told her that they admitted her and that she was on the fourth floor. Maggie took the elevator to the fourth floor. She was very anxious to see Katie or Tony to see what was going on. As she got off the elevator, she could see Tony talking to a nurse at the desk.

"Tony," Maggie called out, "what's going on?"

"They said the baby was in distress and they would have to deliver the baby by giving Katie a c-section. They have to put her out and I was told to stay here. I don't know if she's all right. They won't tell me anything more, Maggie."

"Okay, I'm sure she is fine, and they know what they're doing," Maggie said giving Tony a hug.

An hour had gone by and still no news on Katie and the baby. Tony was beginning to lose it; Maggie could see it in his eyes. Katie meant everything to him and now the baby too. There was only one time when Maggie had felt completely helpless and that was when her dad was sick. Now it was the same thing, there was nothing she could do for Katie.

"Excuse me; we have been waiting for almost two hours. Could you please tell me how Katie Evans is doing?"

"I will see how she is doing and let you know," said the nurse.

"Thank you," said Maggie.

Maggie waited at the desk hoping to get a response. She didn't know what to do for Tony, he was so beside himself. All she could do was try to comfort him and tell him everything would be all right. As she started to head back to Tony the nurse came back to the desk.

"Mrs. Evans is doing well, and the baby is fine and healthy. They just moved them both to room 402. You can go in to see her now.

"Thank you again," said Maggie as she left the nurse's station.

"Tony, come on, Katie's in room 402. We can go see them."

"See them?" Tony said loudly, "them!"

"Yes, Katie and the baby."

They hugged each other and both took a deep breath. They walked to room 402, arm in arm. Tony walked in first. Katie looked so tired but very happy at the same time. Tony gave her a great big hug and a kiss. Beside the bed was a baby bed with the cutest little baby wearing a pink hat and wrapped in a pink blanket. She was beautiful and Tony was grinning from ear to ear. The tension that was in his face had subsided. He looked exhausted as well, for the fear of the unknown had taken a toll on him. He looked at both Katie and the baby and knew what a lucky man he was. Tony put his hand behind the baby's neck and the other hand under the wrapped blanket near the baby's bottom. He was being so careful as not to wake her and brought her close to his chest.

"She's beautiful Katie, you did great," said Tony, smiling at Katie.

"Thanks honey, we did great," said Katie a little groggy.

"Katie, she really is beautiful," said Maggie, "and she looks just like you."

"Would you like to hold her, Maggie?" said Tony.

"I sure would ... come see your aunt Maggie, little one."

Maggie was a natural. She held the baby with such confidence, rocking her back and forth, smiling and giving her little kisses on the forehead.

"Have you thought of a name for her yet?" Maggie asked.

"Yes, her name is Katherine Antonia Evans, Kat for short," said Katie.

"Kat, it's perfect, it suits her, Katie," said Maggie as she looked at the baby. "You've got the best mommy and daddy ever. You're a lucky little girl, Kat," she said as she caressed the baby.

Maggie looked at Katie and Tony and saw how tired they both were.

"I should go and let you two have some alone time and, oh, we will have to get together on a date for a baby shower, once you're feeling up to it Katie. Love you guys and congratulations."

Maggie gave the baby to Katie. She was feeling a little stronger now. Tony watched Katie as she looked at Kat. They were very proud parents. Maggie said her goodbyes and gave both of them a hug. She looked at her watch; she had just enough time to get back to the bakery before closing. She called Julie to make sure she was still there and would fill her in on what had happened when she got to the bakery. Maggie parked her car and went inside to let Julie know what happened.

"Hi, Julie, it's been a long day. Katie and Tony have a baby girl. They named her Kat. She is doing really well. The baby is beautiful, and Tony is a proud dad."

"I'm glad Katie and the baby are okay. What a scare that must have been for them," said Julie.

"Tony was beside himself for sure, and I wasn't much help either. All I could do was be there for him. I'm just glad it turned out the way it did. How was business?"

"Well, business was fantastic. We sold out of everything. I even brought some pies out of the freezer to sell as slices for the customers that came in for coffee and dessert. We will have to do a lot of baking after Thanksgiving to build our stock back up," said Julie.

"Just remember the rule when stock is low," said Maggie. "Whatever we bake for that day we make double; one to sell and one for the freezer. This way we will have a surplus in no time. Our orders, well that's another story. I may have to hire a part-time baker just for orders. It will all work out. I'm just glad we all have a day off."

"Me too," said Julie, "and remember what I said, you're more than welcome to come for Thanksgiving."

"I know, thank you, maybe another time."

"Okay, you know where I live should you change your mind," chuckled Julie. "See you in two days."

"See you Julie, bye."

All Maggie wanted tonight was a good meal and bed. It had been an exhausting, emotional day for her. She locked up and headed through the gate and saw Jasper and Tilly playing. Jasper ran to Maggie's side as soon as he saw her. Tilly was standing there quietly wagging her tail waiting for a petting. Maggie gave her a pat on the head and couldn't believe the change in Tilly. Flora was outside watching them and could see that Maggie was tired. Maggie told Flora about Katie and the baby and that they were fine. The whole situation had put a toll on her and brought back memories of her dad and not being able to help him. Flora gave Maggie a much-needed hug and asked her to stay for supper. Maggie thanked her and said she would take a rain check. Flora smiled and said she understood. Jasper nudging Maggie wanted to go home too. Jasper could sense that Maggie wasn't happy and wanted to be with her.

The drive home was quiet, and Jasper couldn't wait to get inside the house. Maggie went out back and turned on the barbeque. She went back inside and opened the fridge. She brought out two packages of meat and showed Jasper. He knew it wasn't kibble and he was all for it. He started barking and wagging his tail.

"Steak it is, boy."

CHAPTER 17

Katie and the baby were doing really well. Katie was a great mother. Tony hired a cook and housekeeper to take Katie's place at the bed and breakfast. He wanted Katie to focus on Kat. She was her number one priority and Katie didn't want to miss out on the progress Kat was making. She didn't want to miss out on her first smile, her first word or any of the first things that Kat would eventually do. These first moments are so important for a mother to see and hear.

Maggie planned to have Katie's shower on December seventh. After Thanksgiving she sent out the invitations. Katie wanted to have it at the bed and breakfast instead of having it at the church. It made sense to have it there. It would be easier for Katie and the baby. There were 43 people coming to the baby shower. They included friends, aunts, grandmothers, mothers, and cousins. Katie had a large extended family and when you added in Tony's, well it was a lot. Even some people that had stayed at the bed and breakfast wanted to attend Katie's shower. They knew she was having a baby and wanted to be a part of the celebration. Katie wanted to have a suppertime shower, where the guess could enjoy a meal with Katie and the baby. She also wanted to take some of the load from Maggie. It would have been a lot of croissants or fancy bread for 43 people, plus all the desserts. Katie would just have her cook make the meal. Katie had decided on chicken Alfredo penne and a Caesar salad. For dessert she wanted Maggie to make her delicious cheesecakes. Everything was set in motion; the people on the list just had to attend. It was going to be a wonderful shower and the best part of all was them meeting Kat.

The drive-thru was almost finished. The electrical was being hooked up so the speaker and menu board would work. Maggie could have all or just a few items on the board that her customers could ask for. But coffee was definitely number one. Maggie asked Mrs. Murphy to come by tomorrow to be there first drive-thru customer. Tomorrow would be a big day for Magpie Bakery.

With only a few weeks until Christmas, Maggie had a lot of preparing to do, especially her cookies for the town Christmas tree. She also had her plumb pudding pies, which were a must. Since a lot of people had been asking for them already, she has been making them and freezing them. This way her customers can buy them in advance and put them in their own freezer and take them out when needed.

"Maggie," said Ella, "Mark is finished hooking up the speaker and the menu board. Everything is done; the drive-thru is good to go. He wants to show you how to work it."

"That's great Ella, tell Mark I will be right there," said Maggie as she went to get a pad and pen.

She wanted to write his instructions down in case she forgot in the future. Maggie had so much on her mind it was likely to happen. It seemed pretty straightforward, and Mark even helped her run through it with her inside and him ordering. Maggie was amazed at how it worked. She also asked Mark if he would show her how to place the pictures of the items she wanted on the board for customers to order. She had taken pictures of the baked goods and had posters made of each item. The prices were separate in case of price changes. She could put them all on the board or just a few, it was up to her. The one she was most proud of was the coffee cup logo, Magpie. It was a Magpie flying with its wings spread in the center of the cup with the words Magpie Bakery in-between the bird's wings. It looked really nice on the board for everyone to see. Maggie thanked Mark for helping her and asked him to thank Mr. Sands for her. The job everyone did was outstanding and none of her business had stopped or slowed down because of it. She was very grateful to all of them.

"Julie, I have to go out for a bit and I'm taking Jasper too. Flora has to take Tilly for a checkup. I shouldn't be too long."

"All right, we'll be fine."

Maggie changed into the clothes she wore to work and went to get Jasper. Maggie drove into the parking lot of the Sit & Dine Café. She took out Jasper's leash from the glove box. Most of the stores in Carleton Falls were pet friendly, but a leash was definitely expected. In eating establishments pets were only allowed on their patios and there were only two that allowed it.

Betty Derwood was the owner of the café. Her mom used to run it and when she passed on Betty took it over. Betty used to work there after school to help her out. The diner was still in the past with a black and white checkered floor and counters with stainless steel borders around them. There was a very large mirror on the wall behind the counter, which reflected the whole diner. The stools under the counters were covered in red leather and a soda fountain was at the far end of the counter. The booths were made of highly polished wood and the seats were also covered in red leather. Not only did people come for the good food they came to relive, if only for a short time, the good times they had in the past. Some of the younger ones wanted to experience what it was like, and others were reliving memories.

Betty was a very nice, soft-spoken lady that Maggie had known for a long time; she was a couple of grades ahead of Maggie in school. Betty's brother was Maggie's age, and he loved to tease Maggie. Betty would stick up for Maggie and tell him not to, but he never did listen to his big sister. After high school he eventually moved away. He wanted to see the world he would say, and he did. He loved to skate and got hired by a company that performed on ice. He was really good and got to skate in a lot of cities around the world. Now he is married, has two children and lives in Paris. His dream did come true. As for Betty, like Maggie, Carleton Falls was home for her. Her father, Mr. D, the kids would call him, worked at a nursery in Hainesley. He is now retired and Betty and her dad still live in the home she grew up in. They look after each other and if she ever needs help at the café, he is there to help her. He told her he's not much of a cook but he's a darn good dishwasher. Betty and her dad had a great relationship, one that Maggie wished her and her mom had.

Mr. D was spending more time at the café and was always glad to see Maggie and Jasper. Jasper reminded him of a dog he had when he was a kid, they were both the same dog breed and colouring. He told Maggie that his dog was his best friend. He named him Hero, because he meant everything to him.

"Hero knew when school was let out and would bug my mom to let him out of the gate to go meet me," he said. "Every day, without fail he was there. We would walk home together or if I had a baseball game he would help out and gather the balls we missed when the coach pitched them to us before a game. One time he had found a stray kitten stuck under a fence at one of the ball games. He dug her out from under the fence and carried her to my mom. The cat grew up thinking Hero was her mom. We named the kitten Glory. Hero was always on double duty, with Glory and me. Never a happier dog would you ever meet."

Maggie and Jasper went to the back door of the café. Maggie rang the delivery bell and Mr. D came out of the delivery doors. Jasper saw Mr. D and went right to him wagging his tail and nudging him. Mr. D knelt down to pet Jasper and the grin on Mr. D's face was from ear to ear. Maggie could see the memories in Mr. D's eyes. He was reliving his childhood every time he saw Jasper. Mr. D always told Maggie to bring Jasper with her so he could take Jasper for a walk. He didn't have the time to have a pet so Jasper was the next best thing.

"Hi, Maggie, perfect timing. I'm so glad you and Jasper came for a visit," said Mr. D. "I was just going for a break and the deliveries can wait."

"Thanks, Mr. D, I'm supposed to meet a friend here. How's Betty doing?"

"Betty is good; she's in the kitchen cooking. Today seems to be one of our busier days this week so far. You go in, sit down and order. Jasper and I are going for a nice long walk."

"Thanks, Mr. D. I appreciate you watching Jasper for me.

"I think I appreciate it more, Maggie," chuckled Mr. D.

Maggie entered the café and sat down at one of the booths. Betty's friend Nancy was the waitress and has worked for Betty since she took over the café. Nancy took Maggie's order of a BLT on rye and a glass of lemonade. As Maggie had finished ordering, a friend from the Halloween dance and a customer of the bakery walked through the café door.

"Hi, Stew," said Maggie as he hugged her.

The café was pretty much full now. People were coming in carrying their parcels from Christmas shopping. Town Hardware across the street was just as busy, people coming and going.

"Do you happen to have a rod and reel this size; I need it for ice fishing?"

"Yes, I'll show you what we have, sir. We sell a lot of these and they are quite sturdy too."

"Thank you for your help, I appreciate it. This is perfect, I'll take this rod and I really like this reel," he said, looking everything over.

"Is there anything else I can help you with, sir?"

"No, this is everything I need, thank you."

"Great," she said, as she rang up the sale. "Have a nice day and thank you for shopping at Town Hardware."

"Thanks, you have a nice day as well," he said as he left the cashier and headed towards the exit doors."

"Hello, Jack!"

"Oh, hello, Mrs. Murphy," said Jack, startled.

"Jack, it's Ellen, I'm sure we can be on a first name basis."

"Definitely Ellen, how are you?"

"I'm good, always keeping busy. The church always has something going on and I need some display boards. We are having a big fundraiser next Monday for new lighting in the church. There will be food and music. Will you be able to come, Jack?"

"Thanks for the invite, I will be there, what time?"

"It starts at seven."

"Sounds like a good cause, see you then, bye, Ellen."

"Bye, Jack."

Jack went through the exit doors and towards his truck. As he put the rod and reel in the back of his truck, he noticed Maggie and Jasper outside, across the street at the Sit & Dine Café. Maggie was with that Stew guy she was dancing with at the Halloween dance. He hadn't met Stew but Kim had mentioned him. Already Jack didn't like him. They were saying goodbye and hugging each other, then she gave Stew a kiss on the cheek. Jack had bought the rod and reel for Maggie to use at Carleton Falls State Park. He was hoping to show her how to ice fish. The temperature was getting quite cold and soon the river would be frozen at least closer to the shore if not completely in the middle. But seeing them together Jack knew Stew was obviously more to her than just a friend. He slammed the tailgate, wishing he had never come into town.

For the last month he had thought a lot about Maggie and was eventually going to ask her out. But he had other priorities. His mother had become ill and he didn't know if she was going to be all right. He took a leave of absence to spend time with her. She was the only family he had left. His aunt, his mother's sister had passed away two years ago and she never married. His mom was doing much better and he was planning to see her for Christmas. They always spent Christmas together since her sister's passing and he even had her moved to Hainesley, so he could be closer to her. He rented a small apartment for her and could now visit her any time. Jack didn't want to start a relationship with Maggie until he had everything taken care of.

"Jasper, come here!" yelled Maggie as he pulled the leash out of her hand and ran across the street.

Maggie saw it was Jack, and Jasper was all over him, wagging his tail, nudging Jack and even jumping up on him. She walked across the street very happy to see him.

"Hi, Jack, it's been a while, nice to see you."

"Nice to see you too, Maggie," he said as he was petting Jasper.

"How have you been?" said Maggie.

"Busy, and you?" said Jack.

"Yes, busy as well," said Maggie, feeling Jack was just being polite and really didn't want to talk. She felt he was being cold and distant.

"Well, nice to see you, Maggie. I should be getting back. Bye, boy," he said as he gave Jasper one last pat on the head.

"Bye, Jack," Maggie said as she took Jasper's leash in her hand and headed back to her car.

"Get in, boy," she said as she opened the car door wondering what was up with Jack.

She parked the car and took Jasper back to Flora's house all the while thinking, had he met someone and wasn't interested in her after all, or maybe never was. But that couldn't be. He was acting like he was upset with her. Had she done something to annoy him? she wondered. She had just too much on her plate to try and figure it out. She decided not to lose any sleep over it.

Back at the bakery she was still training Anna; she was showing her the different baked goods and the price list. She showed her how to make the coffee and told her the larger items like a whole cake would not be on the menu board for the drive-thru. Anna said she felt confident about tomorrow and was looking forward to it. Maggie had arranged for Mrs. Murphy to be the first drive-thru customer and scheduled it for eight in the morning.

The rest of the afternoon went smoothly. Maggie and Julie made the cheesecakes for Katie's shower and put them in the walk-in. They also made some pies and apple strudel and put them into the freezer as a surplus for customers wanting a baked good with their coffee.

Everyone was getting excited about tomorrow. They had all put in a full day's work today and they all went home to rest up for the big day tomorrow.

CHAPTER 18

Today came early for Maggie and Jasper. Maggie hadn't slept a wink, and Jasper knew Maggie wasn't herself. Maggie spent most of the night tossing and turning, going over the conversation with Jack or the lack of it. Then thinking how different it will be for both herself and her customers having a drive-thru. She hoped that she had made the right decision.

"Eat up boy, time to go."

Hmm . . . Maggie thought as she got in her car. Charlie's car wasn't in his driveway and neither was Mrs. Abigail. It wasn't strange for Mrs. Abigail. If she had a card game at a friend's house, she sometimes stayed the night. But Charlie, very rarely is he up this early, let alone up and gone out. I hope everything is okay she thought.

Maggie had pulled into the parking lot at the back of the bakery. There were cars in most of the parking spaces and even people waiting to get into the bakery. Maggie opened the back gate and Flora was there to greet her and Jasper. Tilly was sitting there calmly waiting as well. Flora asked Maggie what was going on? Maggie didn't know herself but speculated it had something to do with the drive-thru and Mrs. Murphy ordering the first coffee. Flora and Maggie said their goodbyes and Flora took both dogs inside, while Maggie went into the bakery. Julie pulled up as well and went inside. Both Maggie and Julie looked at each other.

"What's going on," said Julie.

"I'm not sure," said Maggie, "but someone is behind this."

Maggie opened the bakery doors, and a crowd of people entered.

Maggie asked why everyone was here so early and Rita, an employee from Town Hardware said Mrs. Murphy told pretty much everyone that Magpie Bakery was having a celebration on the opening of their new drive-thru. Maggie should have guessed it. The girls were also in the bakery now and Anna was looking at the clock, getting ready for Mrs. Murphy to pull up in the drive-thru and order. It was amazing, everyone outside knew what was about to happen. There was even a photographer from the Golden Gazette in Hainesley.

It just turned eight o'clock and it was so quiet you could hear a pin drop. Then came the words, one regular coffee and a strawberry danish please. Anna took the order and handed Mrs. Murphy a regular coffee and a strawberry danish. The whole parking lot cheered and some even honked their horns. A drive-thru was born and the publicity Magpie Bakery was going to get was done solely by one woman, Mrs. Murphy. Now Maggie knew where Mrs. Abigail and Charlie were, outside waving flags with the others. The drive-thru was getting lineups and inside was just as busy. Maggie couldn't wait to see tomorrow's paper. She looked over at Anna. She was taking everything in stride, she wasn't nervous or rushed. She was doing a great job.

By nine o'clock most of the cars in the parking lot had gone and the store was a little calmer. The girls had a moment to breathe and restock some of the baked goods. Anna was making more coffee when there was a lull in drive-thru customers. Which so far wasn't that often, but the drivers waited patiently when she told them, one moment please. Mrs. Abigail and Charlie came into the bakery to congratulate Maggie. Maggie thanked them for coming and sat with them at one of the tables. She asked them what they wanted and Charlie wanted a black coffee and a strawberry scone with whipped cream and Mrs. Abigail wanted a cream puff and a black coffee as well. She came back with their order and told them it was on the house. They both thanked her and smiled. All her regulars showed up and even Tony, Kim and Dale dropped by. Pretty much all of the merchant owners also dropped by or went through the drive-thru and honked their horns. All of this happened because of one lady. A lot of people think Mrs. Murphy is a gossiper but Maggie thinks she talks about people and their situations so she can help them or someone they know. If you don't ask questions then others can't help. She is a very selfless person and Maggie will never forget that.

Just then Mrs. Murphy came in. She sat down with the three of them. She had to drop some things off at the Church for the fundraiser after she had gone through the drive-thru. Maggie thanked her for coming and spreading the word.

Mrs. Murphy looked at all of them and said, "You just have to know the right people to tell and things spread very quickly."

They all laughed and told her, "Well done."

Mrs. Abigail said her goodbyes and Charlie did as well. Maggie reminded Charlie about him and her getting together to make Christmas cookies. He said he would be there with bells on and to just let him know when. With just the two of them sitting there Mrs. Murphy had mentioned that she saw Jack yesterday at Town Hardware. He was very pleasant and she invited him to the fundraiser.

"What did he say to your invitation?" asked Maggie.

"He said he would be going, he's such a nice young man Maggie."

"Yes, he is," said Maggie not wanting to tell Mrs. Murphy how cold he'd been with her.

"I would have thought you two would be together by now."

"Oh Mrs. Murphy, a few dances at a Halloween dance does not make two people boyfriend, girlfriend."

"No, it does not, your right," said Mrs. Murphy, "but the look in your eyes and his when he swept you around the room, does. You'll see, Maggie."

Maggie laughed a little at what Mrs. Murphy said and shrugged her shoulders. She wanted Mrs. Murphy to think that her relationship with Jack was no big deal. But it was really starting to bother

Maggie. She started rehashing things in her head. Her and Jack meet at the dance and they have a great time. He says he will contact her and doesn't. She doesn't hear from him for a month and when she finally sees him, he is abrupt and cold to her. She was never one to chase after a man and certainly wasn't going to start now. Her life was far too busy to pursue a relationship, especially if it was one sided.

"Enjoy your day Maggie, I will be over in a couple of days to pick up the desserts for the fundraiser," said Mrs. Murphy, "and I expect to see you there as well."

Maggie said she would be there and gave Mrs. Murphy a hug and thanked her again for starting the drive-thru off in style. She couldn't wait to see tomorrow's Hainesley Golden Gazette. She went to see how Anna was doing. Anna said it was going well and she hadn't stopped since they opened this morning. Maggie's coffee was a hit. She was selling muffins and danish as well as apple strudel, which Julie had to replenish from the freezer. Thankfully, she took some out of the freezer earlier when she saw all the people. Now they were thawed out and ready to sell with the coffee. The ones she was making were not cooked yet and being their first drive-thru day it was important not to run out of anything. Maggie told Anna to take a break and she would fill in for her. She also told Anna to help herself to a drink and to a pastry if she wanted. The first thing Anna went for was a coffee then a scone. Maggie just smiled.

All her employees are great workers and she would have to do something special for them. She usually gave them a bonus for Christmas, maybe this year it could be a little bigger. Time would tell for sure.

Maggie was also thinking of packaging her grandmother's coffee and selling it in the bakery. This way people could make it at home too. She has so many ideas but lately there didn't seem to be enough hours in a day. After the New Year she would definitely hire another baker to help Julie. This way she could concentrate on the orders and new business deals.

It was getting late and almost time to close. The girls were still busy out front and Maggie wanted Julie to leave and stop by the bank to make a deposit on her way home. Julie was going to Katie's shower tonight and wanted time to sit with her husband and kids before she left. With Julie being gone all day, she always made sure when she went home after work, that she asked her husband and kids how their day went. They needed her interest in their lives and she needed to know they were all okay. She knew communication was so important in a successful relationship.

It was quiet now and the front door locked. The usual lights were left on over the showcase. Maggie brought a change of clothes and would leave from the bakery; there was no sense in going home and coming all the way back to get the desserts for the shower. She packed all of the desserts in the car and poured two coffees and grabbed a box with six raisin bran muffins that she had boxed earlier. Maggie locked the back door and went to get Jasper. She also took a few Jasper cookies which were a hit with Tilly. Maggie testing Tilly with Jasper cookies was a success and concluded that most dogs would love them. Flora thanked Maggie for the coffee and muffins. They both sat outside drinking their coffee and talking about today's events. Flora saw everything from her backyard and couldn't believe the outpour of people and the love and appreciation for Maggie. Flora was thankful for even knowing Maggie and having Jasper around. Tilly, being a handful was too much for Flora to handle, but now she is such a different dog and Jasper was responsible for that. Flora felt blessed for having both of them in her life.

Maggie left Flora and Tilly and went back to the bakery and sat on the back step with Jasper. She had a few more minutes before she had to leave and wanted to spend some quiet time with Jasper. With Jasper at her side Maggie was reflecting on the day's events. She was glad to see Kim and Dale go through the drive-thru and Tony as well. They didn't go in to see her but she saw them through the camera that is installed, plus their horn honking was a total giveaway. She knew she would be seeing Kim at the shower and Tony said he would watch Jasper for her. She was very fortunate to have a great support system from her friends. But it was more than that. It was pretty much the whole town as well. Carleton Falls was home. She always felt planted, in a safe environment. It was the same feeling she had when she went camping. It was the beautiful outdoors, the fresh air, the clear clean water and the peacefulness, everything being in harmony with each other. That was home too. A safe space her and her dad had explored together.

Maggie was thinking of the new, very large cooler she had purchased for the hatchback of her car. The baked goods will stay fresh and cool with it having a temperature control, especially in the warmer months. Today being colder she definitely wouldn't have to worry about it. She had made the cheesecakes in large rectangular pans. This way she would cut them into nice size squares for dessert when she got there. She also made whipping cream to add to each slice and some chocolate drizzle to add over everything. The two pans she made were cherry cheesecake and each pan should give her twenty-four slices. Normally for the bakery she would make round cherry, chocolate, strawberry and plain vanilla cheesecakes. Chocolate was her best seller but Katie's favourite was the cherry.

Sometimes having that quiet moment to regroup her thoughts and just relax was all Maggie needed to finish up her busy day. Finally ready they were off to the bed and breakfast. Maggie pulled into the driveway and parked at the side door. She had forgotten how beautiful the scenery around the bed and breakfast looked at nighttime. It was stunning and all the landscape lights lit up all the flowerbeds. The flowers were mostly gone but the bushes were still showing their fall colours.

As Maggie got out of her car, Tony greeted her.

"What a day you've had, Maggie," said Tony.

"I know, and it's not over," she laughed, "and thanks for coming. I saw you in the drive-thru."

"I wouldn't have missed it and your welcome. So, I have the large dining room set up ready to go. I added two tables and chairs from the small dining room for extra seating. You have a half hour before the guests arrive. I also had a table set up for gifts and a card box just like you wanted. It's now in your hands. Don't forget to enjoy yourself too, Maggie."

"I will Tony, you and Jasper have fun too. Here is some kibble for his supper."

Tony took Jasper to the back of the building for a run. Maggie carried the cakes into the kitchen. There she met with Katie's new cook who was really cooking up a storm. The aroma coming from the kitchen was intoxicating. It was making her so hungry she couldn't wait to eat. As Maggie was cutting her dessert, she introduced herself to the cook. He said he was happy to meet her and that his name was Carter Atson. He said he had worked as a chef for twenty years in a New York upscale restaurant. He was glad a cooking job had become available in Carleton Falls. He wanted to find a more relaxing environment to work in. In New York it was quite a hectic pace and after twenty years he had had enough. Right now, he was staying in one of the bed and breakfast rooms. He wanted to rent something in town but nothing was available. He said Katie negotiated the room in with his pay. It was a spare room with ensuite that wasn't being used by the guests. The room was quite large and with only a double bed in the room he could also have a little sitting area. It was perfect for him since he had never married and was on his own. Maggie welcomed him to Carleton Falls and said she was glad to meet him. Having finished cutting the cheesecakes into slices, she placed them in the fridge until dessert time.

Maggie headed to the large dining room to greet the guests. Kim and Julie were the first ones through the doorway. Maggie gave them a quick hug and Liz and Ella were next. She instructed the guests to put all the gifts on the table that Tony provided. There were a lot of family members attending, especially on Tony's side that Maggie had never met. Everyone was now seated and Katie came into the room with a bassinet on wheels. Katie had just finished feeding Kat and she was taking a nap. Katie walked around the room pushing the bassinet letting each person have a look at the baby. Everyone pretty much said the same thing, she was beautiful. Katie sat down with the bassinet beside her and Maggie let Carter know they were ready for the meal. He brought out a cart with bowls of chicken Alfredo. He pushed the cart to each table and put two bowls of food on each one. The guest could put the amount of food they wanted on their plates and pass the bowl around. He only had to make three trips to the kitchen. Maggie had grabbed another cart and placed a large bowl of Caesar salad on each table. The dining room was very quiet. Everyone was enjoying the meal. On each table Maggie had put two bottles of wine.

Katie looked at Maggie and smiled. Everything was perfect.

Maggie helped clear the tables with Carter. It didn't take long as people went to talk to Katie and see the baby. While Carter was on the last couple of tables, Maggie went to put the coffee on and took out the sliced cheesecakes, whipping cream and chocolate drizzle from the fridge. She laid out the plates on the two food carts. On each plate she put a slice of cheesecake and a nice dollop of whipping cream. Her chocolate drizzle was in a piping bag ready for the finishing touches. With the top of the cart and a shelf on the bottom, Maggie was able to get half of the desserts on each cart. It didn't take Maggie long and while she was busy Katie was talking to her guests about her ordeal at the hospital. She also talked about Kat and what a good baby she was and how much she was enjoying motherhood. Maggie took her seat beside Katie. Everyone had their dessert and complimented Maggie on the delicious cheesecake. Carter had put two pitchers of coffee on each table with bowls of cream, milk and sugar. Some were enjoying the wine so much they didn't want coffee and a few had asked for tea. All in all, the night was really going well.

Katie's mom was asking Katie if Kat made pouty faces at bathtime. Katie asked her how she knew. It seems Kat was just like her mother. Some of the guests were telling Katie of their own experience with their children as babies. They pretty much told her that with the first baby it was a learning process for the mother. Not all babies were the same when it came to their eating and sleeping habits. While everyone was sharing their experiences with babies and their children, Maggie and Carter had resumed their roles in clearing off the tables. Carter left a pot of coffee in case someone wanted another cup.

Maggie took a chair over to the table with the gifts for Katie. Katie pushed the bassinet over to the table and sat down. Maggie gave her a large wrapped gift and Katie took off the card and read it out loud. She then proceeded to open it up. It was a beautiful baby swing from Tony's mom that would come in very handy for Katie when Kat needed to be rocked to sleep. With each gift Katie opened she tried to hold back the tears. Everyone had been so generous. She got bedding for Kat's crib and lots of cute baby clothes and some onesies. She got a beautiful stroller from her mother that would come in handy for walks around the bed and breakfast and a few photography sessions for now and when Kat gets older. There were lots of diapers, baby wash and bath products and lotions. Baby towels, wash clothes, baby bottles, were also given. Two people had given a car seat and a baby carrier, something that Katie hadn't even thought of yet. She was given a lot of gift cards and money to buy what she needed for Kat. Babies grow fast and Katie could buy some larger clothes when they were needed. Someone even opened a bank account for Kat and put some money into it to get her started. Katie had a date already set up for her and the person to go to the bank together and put it in Katie's name until Kat was older.

Katie was overwhelmed with everything she got for Kat. She thanked everyone for coming and said that they were welcome to come and visit her and Kat anytime. One at a time they came up and gave Katie a hug and took another look at Kat. They congratulated her on a beautiful daughter and some of the family members even offered to babysit when she needed some time for herself. It was a very nice shower and everyone enjoyed themselves. Kat was just waking up from her nap as the last person had left. Katie was getting tired herself and enjoyed every minute of the shower. She thanked Maggie for arranging it all and congratulated Maggie on the success of the drive-thru. She heard all about it from Tony and he told her a photographer from the newspaper Golden Gazette was there as well. Katie gave Maggie a big hug and a kiss on the cheek.

"You deserve good fortune and so much more," she told Maggie. "I hope you find what I have," said Katie.

"Maybe someday, Katie," said Maggie. "I'm pretty satisfied with the way things are right now."

"I know," said Katie, "but some day you will meet someone to share all your accomplishments with."

Maggie smiled. "Maybe, but for now I need to check and see if Carter needs any help."

Katie took Kat and went to find Tony, to let him know Maggie was leaving. Maggie went to see

Carter. He had everything cleaned up and put away. He certainly was an excellent chef and they were lucky he applied for the job. Maggie said good bye to Carter and told him she enjoyed working with him tonight. She waited outside by her car to get some fresh air. She was getting tired as well and it had been a very long day. Tony opened the door and out ran Jasper. Maggie gave him a hug and opened the car door. Into the passenger seat he went waiting for Maggie to get into the car. Tony thanked Maggie for all she did and how much he and Katie appreciated it. Kat got a lot of wonderful gifts. Maggie said she enjoyed it too and mentioned that the baby swing might come in handy tonight for Katie. She told Tony that Kat had slept most of the night at the shower and that Katie was tired. Tony said he would set it up and keep an eye on Kat so Katie could have a sleep. Katie and Tony are a great couple, always looking out for each other. Maggie said good night to Tony and drove home anticipating a quick hot bath before bed. Jasper so tired from his run at the bed and breakfast fell right to sleep on his comfy dog bed. Maggie smiled and got into bed. It didn't take long and she was fast asleep too, both of them having had a very exhausting day.

CHAPTER 19

"Hmm ..." said Maggie as she stretched and rolled over in bed.

That was Jasper's cue to jump on the bed and lick Maggie's face.

"Okay boy, I'm awake," she said petting Jasper on the head. "I really need to train you to make coffee," she laughed, "or at least invest in a coffee maker with a timer on it."

All Jasper was interested in was breakfast and for Maggie to get up. Maggie got up out of bed and searched for her slippers. Jasper loved to take Maggie's slippers and put them in his dog bed. He never chewed on them, he just liked laying on them. Maggie thought it was like a security blanket for Jasper, like having Maggie with him all night.

"Here, boy," she called, as Jasper came running to his bowl. "Take your time Jasper; we're in no rush this morning."

Maggie took a sip of her coffee as she looked out the front window. She noticed frost on the roofs across the street and some on the windshield of her car. Time to get the scraper out of the hatchback of the car and put it in the back seat she thought. You just never know when Carleton Falls was going to have snow. Christmas was getting closer every day. Sometimes they got snow in December and other times it waited until January. Either way the temperature was quite cold. Maggie took another sip of her coffee and saw the newspaper delivery guy delivering her paper. She took off her slippers and put on her shoes that were in the hall closet. With her robe on, she walked as quickly as she could to the curb to retrieve the paper from her mailbox. It seemed everyone else was still in bed as the houses around didn't have any lights on. It would be nice to go back to bed Maggie thought, but today she was going to make some Jasper cookies and take them over to Pet Start. They had agreed to take some dog cookies on consignment and see how they sell. The owners, Sherry and Leo Blackly had a few more stores in different towns and cities. If the cookies sold in this store, Sherry said she would take some for their other stores. Maggie had stickers made up to put on the packages. The logo was a white oval with a silhouette of a dog with the words Jasper Cookies written in black along the top inside the oval. Each package would be tied with a ribbon that looks like a dog collar and a dog tag showing the healthy ingredients. On the back of the package at the bottom Maggie would put a sticker saying, made at Magpie Bakery, Carleton Falls.

Once back inside Maggie put her slippers on, and picked up her coffee cup she had left on the hall table. Taking a sip, she went into the kitchen with Jasper following her. She unrolled the paper and saw her bakery on the front page. Wow, she thought, never would she have thought it would be on the front page. It was a 5 x 7 size picture with a lengthy write up. It was a really nice picture with all the cars and people standing out front next to the drive-thru cheering and waving flags. The heading was Coffee and a Danish to Go. It mentioned the owner Maggie Sinclaire of Magpie Bakery in Carleton Falls and why the drive-thru was added to the bakery. It goes on to mention the town's people and how supportive everyone was. It even listed the kind of baked goods you could purchase. At the end of the article it said, continue on page two. Maggie flipped over the page and there was another picture. This one showed Mrs. Murphy ordering from her car window in the drive-thru. This is great Maggie thought. Mrs. Murphy deserved the recognition. She was the one that orchestrated everything. Maggie was so happy and had a feeling; things were going to get really busy.

Maggie made herself another coffee. She needed a little more time to look at the paper and look at what her bakery had become. It was a dream she had all along and now it was out there in the public's eye, even further than she had expected, all the way to Hainesley and beyond. Their paper went to all the small towns in the area. This was definitely a big deal, her grandmother's coffee was going to be a big hit and packaging it would be even bigger. It was so overwhelming for Maggie her head was starting to spin. She needed to calm down and take one step at a time. First, Jasper Cookies and then Alice's Coffee.

Maggie got dressed and put on a warm jacket. She opened the car door for Jasper and he went to the passenger seat. Maggie also put into the car a bag of clothing to keep at the bakery for changing into when she was working. She also took her snowbrush and windshield scraper from her hatchback and put it into the back seat. Maggie got in and started the car. She turned on the button for heated seats and the heated air for the windshield. It didn't take long for the window to be clear of frost and their seats nice and warm. All buckled up, off she drove to the bakery and a brand-new day.

The bakery parking lot was full and the drive-thru was lined up from the drive-thru window, through the parking lot and down the street. Yep, it's going to be a busy day. I'm so glad I put a sign in the window for a baker wanted, days ago she thought, there's no way it could wait until the New Year. Maggie and Jasper headed to the back gate. Flora met Maggie and took Jasper. She congratulated Maggie on the write-up and was very happy for her new found friend. Even before Maggie could even get inside the bakery people were honking their horns. It seems everyone in Carleton Falls had read the morning paper.

"Good morning, Julie, it's going to be a hectic day," said Maggie.

"It already is," laughed Julie, "we have already sold out of danish. I put strudel on the board instead, at least until I bake some more."

"My appointment with Pet Start isn't until late afternoon, so I'll bake some danish while I'm making some Jasper cookies. You carry on with your orders, Julie."

Julie looked a little flushed in the face, Maggie could see today was taking a toll on Julie. Maggie decided to make a phone call.

"Good morning, I hope I didn't wake you."

"No, no, I was up, everything okay, Maggie?"

"With the photo of the bakery in the newspaper, we are really busy and could use an extra hand, if you're up to it."

"Yes, I saw the photo and the great write up. I will be there as soon as I can, bye."

Maggie went out front to see how the girls were doing. It was literally all hands-on deck. The line up at the counter was just as busy as the drive-thru. The table and chairs were full as well. Looks like everyone decided to come to Magpie for their morning coffee and pastry. Liz was great with the counter and getting orders ready to go, pretty much what Anna was doing with the drive-thru. Ella was good at serving the sit-down customers in the bakery. This will work out great she thought, pondering the idea in her head as she went over to talk to Liz. As Liz left the counter area to see Julie, Maggie filled in.

"Great write-up in the paper, Maggie," said Mr. Brown, sitting at one of the tables. He was the vanilla slice guy that comes on the same day, never orders anything else and never stays to eat it in the bakery.

"Thanks, Mr. Brown, it was a beautiful write-up and all because of Mrs. Murphy," said Maggie. "Can I get anything else for you?"

"Yes thanks, I'll take two of your cinnamon raisin bagels with cream cheese, and another regular coffee to go."

Maggie had Ella ring in his order while she was getting it ready.

"Here you are, Mr. Brown. Have yourself a great day and thanks for stopping by," said Maggie.

As Mr. Brown left, Charlie had come through the front doors.

"Wow, you weren't kidding, quite the turn over today, Maggie."

"Thank you for coming Charlie; here I have an apron for you and a hair net. Ella, Charlie is going to help you serve the customers and Liz is in the back helping Julie. If you could ring the orders in for Charlie that would be great, then Charlie can stick to getting the order ready."

Ella nodded her head as she was boxing a round vanilla cake.

"Glad to have you aboard, Charlie," she said.

Charlie was great with people and if he was a little slow with an order, Maggie new with his easy disposition, the customer wouldn't mind. He could be a charmer with the ladies, if he wanted to be. He would be a good catch for any of them. But Maggie thought he was still in love with Sue and waiting for her to return from Italy. Maybe that's why she left. She was worried about losing another person she loved. Maggie hoped that someday her mother would return and get together with Charlie.

Maggie went back to the kitchen to bake some danish pastries. Danish pastry dough like croissant dough needed resting periods after each fold and for final proofing. Also, like croissants they were made in a two-day process then put into the freezer. Danish pastry dough contained eggs whereas croissant dough did not. Maggie took out a box of danish from the freezer, put them on cookie sheets and let them sit while she was getting the fillings from the walk-in. They usually made strawberry, cherry, blueberry and lemon danish. Maggie placed the various fillings in the middle of the partially thawed pastry, and then brushed on an egg wash glaze over the exposed pieces of pastry. Into the oven they went while Maggie made a powdered sugar glaze to drizzle over the danish pastries after they were cooked and cooled.

Julie had just finished packing up the orders for the day and gave them to a delivery guy at the side door, one less thing to deal with. While Julie was showing Liz what to make next, Maggie needed to get her Jasper cookies made. They needed time to cool and be packaged. Julie looked less stressed now and Liz was good at picking things up quickly. Julie would show her a recipe and together they would make the same thing side by side. This would give Liz confidence in what she was making because she could watch Julie as well. The best part was that there would be a double batch made. The danish pastries were out of the oven and onto the cooling racks. In went the Jasper cookies, three trays with two dozen cookies on each tray. That will give her six dozen cookies all packaged in half dozen bags. If this turned out well with Pet Start selling her Jasper Cookies, she would try out her other recipe for dog bites; a vegetable-based dog snack. If Jasper and Tilly like them, then in theory all dogs should like them. It's just whether there was a market for them.

Charlie came to the back to let Maggie know everything was going really well out front. Maggie thanked him again and sent Charlie out front with some more danish pastries.

"Smells so good," said Charlie.

"You help yourself to anything you want, Charlie and a drink too. When you get a minute take a break and maybe you can relieve Ella as well."

"Thanks, Maggie and don't you worry about a thing. Ella and I are doing great out there. Just keep the baked goods coming. Oh, we are a little short on layer cakes as well. Ella just sold the last one."

"We have some in the walk-in, Charlie. I will bring some out to you."

First Maggie pulled out the Jasper cookies to cool on the racks. Then Maggie went and got two cakes from the walk-in and took them out front. Business was slowing down but Anna was still going steady. She placed the cakes in the showcase as she watched Ella and Charlie teasing each other. Maggie knew Charlie would have a good time. Since he wanted to help out before maybe he could come more often, she thought, as she still needed to make Christmas cookies for the Carleton Falls Town Square Christmas tree event and could use another person in the bakery. She would think about it because it was really another baker she needed, but for now she went over to give Anna a break.

"Everything going all right, Anna?" asked Maggie.

"It's really going well, it's steady and I really don't have time to think about anything. I just pour the coffee and bag a baked good and on to the next one."

"Are you enjoying it, Anna? I guess what I'm asking is, do you like working here?"

"Yes, very much, I like to keep busy and so far, it's been very busy. This is home for me now. I'm here as long as you want me, Maggie."

Maggie smiled, gave Anna a hug and thanked her for doing a great job. While Maggie watched the drive-thru Anna went to get something to eat and a drink. She introduced herself formally to Charlie and welcomed him here. It was nice to hear the laughter in the bakery. The tensions were low and everyone could breathe. The bakery was half full now and the drive-thru although steady was a slower pace as well. Mostly just coffee for those who needed caffeine to get them through the day. Maggie figured it would pick up again when people got off work and needed a coffee heading home.

It was two o'clock and everything was good out front. Maggie needed to get her Jasper Cookies packaged for her visit to Pet Start.

"Six in here and six in this one and that's it. Now for the dog collar ties and the dog tags," said Maggie to herself.

Maggie boxed all of the Jasper Cookies ready to go to Pet Start. She wanted to take a break and ask Charlie if he would like to join her. I'm sure he could use another break by now, she thought. Maggie peeked out front and got Charlie's attention. She had grabbed a coffee for both of them, waiting for him to come back and join her sitting at the lunch table.

"Thank you very much for helping me out today, Charlie. You're the greatest," said Maggie.

"You're welcome, any time, Maggie, I really enjoyed myself today. I met a lot of people I haven't seen in years. I often wondered what happened to Ross Ranner."

"Who is Ross Ranner?" Maggie asked as she took a sip of her coffee.

"He was a guy that followed me around from job to job, until I got the job with the computer software company. A royal pain in the ... well, you know the kind, I'm sure Maggie. He was an R & R guy. A rules and regulations guy, he would call himself, because he had two Rs in his name. What a joke that was. He followed me to two different jobs I had. The first job I left just to get away from him. Then he showed up at my second job. Probably saw the same help wanted ad. He thought he was going to ride on my coat tails. He would get in the boss's face and say I wasn't doing my job. He would say all the work was left for him or the person that came in after me. He must have complained to the boss so much that the owner came in one day to see how my day was going. I showed him the work I had done and a list of the accounts I got for the company. He was really impressed and saw that I was more valuable to him in a different department. I was now Mr. R & R's boss. Needless to say, Mr. R & R was let go. This job helped me get to the computer software job."

"Wow, Charlie, he must have been surprised to see you working in a bakery."

"Yes, he was, but I told him I flew in to help a friend and would be going back to the Bahamas shortly," laughed Charlie. "It's not that I can't go to the Bahamas, I just rather stay here."

"You're just too funny, Charlie. Did you find out what he does for a living?

"No, he didn't say and I didn't ask. But he was very polite when we were talking, so I think he had learned a lesson or two through the years. He did tell me he lives in Wesbridge and moved there a few years ago. He saw the bakery write-up in the paper and wanted to check it out. You just never know who you're going to meet."

"It sounds like you had an enjoyable day, Charlie."

"I did Maggie, and I can't wait to help you make cookies either."

"Probably next week, Charlie."

"Perfect, just give me a call and oh, a young man came into the bakery and left a résumé," said Charlie as he searched for it in his pocket, then handed it to Maggie.

Maggie unfolded the paper and slowly read it. She was very impressed and told Charlie she would call him tomorrow. Maggie told Charlie she had to leave and go to the pet store. Charlie said he would stay until the bakery closed and not to worry about Jasper. He would pick him up at Flora's house and take him home. Maggie called Flora to let her know, as she hadn't met Charlie yet. She knew Flora would like him as much as she did.

Maggie packed her car with the cookies and headed to Pet Start. Once inside she saw Sherry and showed her the Jasper Cookies. There were a few customers inside the store buying pet food. One lady even remarked on the cookies and wanted to buy a package for her dog. Maggie and Sherry had already talked about pricing when they met last time. It was an instant sale and the smile on Sherry's face was a good thing. Maybe there was a market for Jasper Cookies after all. Maggie thanked Sherry and if all the cookies sold, Sherry would call Maggie for another order. Maggie left Pet Start and drove into Hainesley for supplies. She needed to make the desserts for the church fundraiser, tomorrow night. Mrs. Murphy was going to pick them up and she wanted to make them first thing in the morning. Since Charlie was going to watch Jasper, she didn't need to hurry.

CHAPTER 20

There was no time to waste this morning, Maggie made herself a coffee and Jasper was eating his kibble. Maggie needed to lay out the clothes she wanted to wear at the fundraiser. Should she dress up for the fundraiser? why not, she thought. There will probably be a lot of people there tonight. She took out a pair of black faux-leather pants and a long-sleeved ivory cashmere sweater. The weather was getting colder and a pair of leather ankle boots would do just fine. She packed them in a duffle bag with some makeup and a comb. Now, to take a quick shower and get Jasper over to Charlie's house. She must remember to take some kibble as well.

Charlie was up waiting for Jasper and when Maggie dropped him off, he told her to enjoy herself at the Fundraiser. If she got home too late it was all right if Jasper stayed with him overnight. This took a big load off of Maggie's shoulders, knowing Jasper was taken care of. Charlie mentioned Flora and what a sweetheart she was. He told Maggie he would drop Jasper at Flora's house this morning and stay to visit. They both got along really well and the stories she told him about Tilly and Jasper was incredible, he thought. Looking at Tilly he would never have known she had an anxiety issue. Maggie smiled and agreed at how well

Tilly was doing and a new friend she had also made, knowing Flora.

Maggie left Charlie's and headed to work with the supplies she had picked up last night still in her car. The weather was cold so they were fine in her car overnight. The parking lot was almost as busy as yesterday and the drive-thru was the same, quite busy. These were the coffee drinkers wanting their first cup of morning coffee and didn't have time to make it at home. I really need to get grandmother's packaged coffee in the store for customers to buy and make at home, she thought. There was no time to think of it now, but definitely a future project. Maggie made a few trips to her car and brought all the supplies in as the girls were busy with the customers and orders. The first thing on her agenda was the desserts for the fundraiser.

She decided to make trays of cherry and blueberry tarts. This wouldn't take her too long. Into the mixer the ingredients went. Maggie rolled out the dough and cut circles the size she needed for each tart. Her tart trays held twenty individual tarts. She decided to make four trays. She placed each circle size piece of dough into the individual tart space and pushed the dough into the bottom of the mould and up the sides. When two trays were ready, she put them into the oven and continued working on the other two.

"What have you decided on for the next dessert?" Julie asked.

"I thought I would make pineapple cheesecake squares," said Maggie.

"I'll make some of the Graham cracker base for you and I'm thinking you'll want three trays?"

"Yes, that would be great, Julie, thank you."

While Julie was spreading the crumbled cracker base over the three trays, Maggie was finishing the last two tart trays. She took out the two that were ready and put the final two into the oven. The first two were put on the cooling racks then Maggie started on the cheesecake ingredients while waiting for the last two tart trays. When Julie finished her trays, she took out the tarts from the oven to cool and popped hers into the other oven on medium heat. This helped the Graham cracker base to set better. After only a few minutes Julie took them out of the oven and placed the trays on the racks to cool. Maggie was almost ready to fill the trays Julie made with the Graham cracker base.

"Looks good Maggie, and smells yummy," said Julie watching Maggie spread the cream cheese mixture over the Graham cracker mix.

As one tray was filled Julie took it and put it into the walk-in while Maggie did the next one. It certainly was team work as the two of them pressed on to get the desserts made for Mrs. Murphy coming after lunch to pick them up. The cheesecake trays were done and, in the walk-in, now it was time to put the filling into the tarts. Maggie did the two trays with cherry filling and Julie did the other two with blueberry filling. When they were finished the girls packed them in boxes. Over the bottom layer they inserted little stands that they could put cake board on. This made a shelf for the second layer and repeated it for a third layer. With four boxes used, the tarts were ready. Julie and Maggie placed them at the side entrance where it was cooler and away from the kitchen.

Maggie headed to the walk-in to get one cheesecake tray, as Julie answered the bakery phone.

"Yes, we can have those done for you, say around three o'clock. See you then, thank you, I will let Maggie know, bye. Maggie, that was Sherry from Pet Start. She wants to order more Jasper Cookies and will be here around three to pick them up."

"Nice and so unexpected, that's great news," said Maggie. "How many packages did she order?"

"She ordered fifteen packages, which is times six, which is ninety cookies," Julie chuckled. "I better get started on them."

"I need to call the young man who left his résumé yesterday with Charlie. The workload is really increasing and we need some help," said Maggie as she carried on with the cheesecake tray.

She cut the tray into square slices. After it was all sliced, she added crushed pineapple to the top and put it back into the walk-in. She did the same for the other two trays. She got forty square slices from each tray. All she needed to do was box them to go. This way Mrs. Murphy could keep them in the refrigerator in the church kitchen and take out what she needed.

She decided to call Noah Daniels, the young man that had left a résumé. It was important to hire someone and she didn't want to lose this potential employee, especially if he was an experienced baker as his résumé would suggest.

"Hello, is this Noah Daniels?"

"Yes, it is."

"Hi, I'm Maggie Sinclaire, from Magpie Bakery. You left a résumé the other day. Would you be interested in coming in for an interview today?"

"Yes, I would, thank you."

"Shall we say, three o'clock?"

"That would be great."

"See you then, bye," said Maggie as she redialed the phone.

"Hi, Mr. D, it's Maggie, any chance getting five chicken sandwiches and five orders of fries delivered?"

"Your timing is perfect Maggie, I have another delivery and will drop yours off on the way," replied Mr. D.

"Thank you so much, see you soon."

Maggie went out front to check on the girls. Liz was boxing up some strudel and Ella was talking to a customer that was ordering a cake. Anna was busy pouring coffee and bagging a danish. It seemed steady today but certainly not rushed like it was when the news article came out. There were a couple of tables empty but that could change any minute. Maggie saw Ted Mason eating a cream cheese bagel and having a coffee.

"Hello, Mr. Mason, nice to see you."

"Hello, Maggie, how are you?"

"I'm good, things are really . . . busy," she chuckled. "I will be by for some more apples next week. The apple strudel is selling really well as are the apple tarts and the apple pies. Hmm . . . could it be your apples, Mr. Mason?"

"Probably a combination of my apples and your wonderful baking skills," Mr. Mason said kindly. "You're very busy right now Maggie, I will get Jimmy to deliver some to you next week. He has a delivery in Wesbridge next week and can stop by here on his way."

"That would be great, thank you very much," said Maggie as she watched a young man enter the bakery and go to the counter."

As she said goodbye to Mr. Mason, she looked at her watch. It was three o'clock. The young man was right on time. His sandy-coloured hair was shoulder length and he was close to six feet tall. His coat covered up his physique, but he seemed to be medium build. He looked around Maggie's age or younger but she always found it hard to guess peoples ages. It didn't really matter as long as he could do the job. Maggie went over to greet the young man, as he was having a conversation with Liz.

"Hello, are you Noah Daniels?" she asked, as she walked up to the counter.

"Yes, I am, nice to meet you, Miss Sinclaire."

"Please, Maggie is fine and I see you have met Liz."

"Yes, I used to work in my mom's bakery growing up and we were talking about the bagels and how store bought can't compare to freshly baked."

"Why aren't you working there now Noah did your mom close up her bakery? I see your résumé says you have been working casual as a cook at the Parker Alexander Fine Dining Restaurant."

"Just after high school my mom sold the bakery. She wanted to pursue her passion for art and with the selling of the bakery she could do that and with some of the money she received she sent me to culinary school. My passion is baking first and cooking second. I was fortunate to be hired as a cook by Mr. Alexander."

"Mr. Alexander is a nice man to work for, why would you leave him and want to work for me?" asked Maggie, hoping Mr. Alexander wouldn't be upset with her since he orders from her. She didn't want any conflicts.

"The hours of work at the restaurant are not enough for me. It doesn't cover my rent, so I have a second job cleaning at a hotel. Cleaning is not my passion although a necessity. If I can have a chance to bake again, I would gladly take it and hopefully be full time," said Noah.

"How do you think Mr. Alexander would take it, you leaving him?"

"We have talked about it before. He knows I'm looking for full time and would give it to me if he could. He also knows my passion is baking and he's not into that. Every night I see him he asks me if I've found anything. Then one night he told me about your help wanted sign in your window. He saw it when he picked up his cheesecake order. He was the one who told me to put in a résumé. He likes you a lot Maggie and thinks you are a good businesswoman and a great baker as well. So, he would be happy for both of us."

"Come with me, Noah, I would like you to meet our head baker."

Julie was almost finished with the Jasper Cookie order. She was packaging the last one. The next thing to do was to box the pineapple cheesecake squares for Mrs. Murphy. She went to get the boxes from the storage room and returned to see Maggie and Noah standing there.

"Julie this is Noah Daniels, he would like to be a baker here. As head baker I would like you to have some input in Noah working with us," said Maggie.

"Nice to meet you, Noah, I'm sure you have experience. Otherwise, Maggie would not be introducing us."

"Yes, I do, and nice to meet you, Julie."

"My only concern, Noah, is that we do things our way, would you be able to do things our way if it's different from the way you are used to doing them?"

"Yes, I don't have a problem following directions, and most bakers do things in a similar way. They might put a twist on some recipes, but mostly the ingredients to make the baked goods are the same. I would like the chance to work with you, Julie."

"Perfect," said Julie. I will let you and Maggie discuss your hours and your start date while I box these squares."

Maggie and Noah stood talking about his hours. Maggie wanted him to come in at the same time as Julie and leave when she did. As for start date, she could use him starting tomorrow, but he would have to find a place to rent in Carleton Falls. He was renting a small house apartment in Hainesley and could leave anytime as he never signed a lease. The owner knew it was getting too expensive for Noah and would have no trouble renting it, seeing it was a prime location. Maggie advised him to call Bill Rowen, and told him he was the local real estate agent. Noah wanted to start right away. He told Maggie he would commute until he could find something closer. Both of them seemed happy with the agreement. Noah was starting tomorrow and would let Mr. Alexander know tonight. Finally, when Mr. Alexander asks him if he had any luck, he could say yes.

Noah left and Maggie was helping the girls out front. The aroma of fries filled the bakery. Mr. D had dropped off the fries and sandwiches to Maggie. She instructed Liz, Ella and Anna to go and have lunch with Julie in the back. She said she would watch the front and eat later. If she needed any help, she would call them. There were people in the bakery but they had already been served and were eating at the tables. It was only the drive-thru she would have to deal with for now.

A half hour had gone by and Maggie was still doing well juggling the drive-thru and the front counter. Liz, Ella and Anna were standing there nodding their heads, all in agreement at the good job their boss was doing. Each one of them also thanked Maggie for a delicious lunch.

"Your lunch is waiting for you, Maggie," said Liz.

"Thanks Liz, I could use a break," Maggie said, smiling.

Maggie went to go and eat. Julie was just finishing up her lunch.

"When is Noah starting, Maggie?"

"How do you know he's hired?"

"Maggie, I have known you a long time. First of all, he's good looking, second, he's worked in a bakery and third, he's the only one that applied. So, it stands to reason that you hired him, plus those big blue eyes were quite fetching."

"Yes, your right, about everything," laughed Maggie. "I just hope he works out for both of us. He seems like a very nice person."

"Hello, anybody here," called out Mrs. Murphy as she came into the back room.

"Hi, Mrs. Murphy, all the desserts are ready and waiting for you at the side entrance," said Maggie.

"Thanks dear, and you are coming to the fundraiser, correct?"

"Yes, we're all going," said Maggie, "Julie and the girls as well."

"Perfect, I'll see you all tonight. I've got to go; I have lots to do before the event."

"I'll help you out with the desserts, Mrs. Murphy," said Julie.
"Thanks, hun, I appreciate it."

CHAPTER 21

The afternoon was going by really fast. Sherry from Pet Start had come by for the Jasper Cookies and told Maggie her customer's dogs loved their new snack. They even like the packaging. Some people bought them as a gift for their friend's dog. Sherry thanked Maggie and told her she could see herself ordering for her other stores in the New Year. Maggie was so happy to hear that. She thanked Sherry for allowing her to sell them in her store.

Julie and Maggie made a few more cakes for tomorrow and a few more pies before the end of the work day. Both were tired but were looking forward to a night out. Maggie locked up as she said bye to Julie and the others. She said she would see them there, around seven.

Maggie walked into the walk-in and retrieved a bottle of wine, a full-bodied red wine. She also put a roast beef TV dinner into the oven. They did come in handy once in a while. The mere thought of a TV dinner took her back to her grandmother. Alice used to make her own TV dinners. She would cook roast beef, mashed potatoes and corn for a family meal. Plus, she would make gravy from the drippings left in the pan. She would take the leftovers and put them into foil pans that had divided sections. A few slices of roast beef were put into the large section. The next was the mashed potatoes and the third spot was for the corn. She took an ice cube tray and poured the gravy into it and placed it into the freezer. When the gravy was frozen, she would take the cubes, divide them up and put them in plastic bags. The foil trays were covered with foil and place into the freezer, as well as the bags of gravy. When you didn't have time to cook a meal there was always a nutritious meal waiting in the freezer. Pop it into the oven and place the gravy cubes into a pot. Heat everything up and you had a delicious home-cooked meal. Those were good times that Maggie remembered. The roast beef was succulent; each bite mouthwatering and tender. The mashed potatoes were whipped to perfection with a little milk and butter. They were whipped so smooth they melted in your mouth. The combination of meat, whipped potatoes with gravy and corn on your fork was a mouthful of delicious pleasure. You took your time to finish the meal and you did finish it all because you didn't want anything to go to waste. You appreciated the love that went into it in the first place. Back then grandmothers knew how to do everything; they had to for their families.

Maggie was well into her store-bought TV dinner. Nothing like her grandmothers but it filled an empty spot. The glass of wine went down good too. Time to change and get ready for the fundraiser, she thought. First her black faux-leather pants, then her soft ivory sweater. To complete the look, she put on her black leather ankle boots. She took her time and decided to have another glass of wine, while she was getting ready. She was going to walk to the event so a second glass of wine wasn't going to hurt. Her hair was still nicely curled, so she didn't have to touch it up. She decided to add a little makeup to her look. She brushed a little bit of blush on her cheeks, although with the wine making her a little flushed, she probably didn't need it. She then added a touch of lipstick and her look was complete.

She looked at her watch and it was already seven. She made sure all the ovens were turned off then she put on her coat and grabbed her keys and purse. Maggie locked the back door and started to walk over to the church leaving her car at the bakery. The night air was cold and brisk. Maggie busy inside never noticed it was snowing. It must have started an hour ago because there was already some covering the roads. She took her time and made it to the church. The parking lot was full. A great turn out she thought, just what Mrs. Murphy was hoping for. The music was loud in the auditorium and in some of the other rooms they had auctions. Most of the businesses donated to the fundraiser. Again Mrs. Murphy saw to that. She had a way of asking people for things she wanted and everybody admired her for that.

Maggie went into one of the auction rooms. Up for auction was an ice hut. Ice fishing at Carleton Falls State Park was a big deal in the winter months, as well as skating and snowmobiling. Two hundred, Maggie heard someone call out. Looking over she saw Jack. He was bidding on the ice hut with another guy. It was Dale, Kim's husband.

"Two hundred and fifty," called Dale.

"Three hundred," called Jack as he waited for Dale to call three hundred and fifty.

"Going once, twice, three times, sold for three hundred dollars," said the auctioneer.

All participants were asked to collect and pay for their item after each winning bid. This way if anyone decided they didn't want the item, it could be reauctioned at the end of the evening. Jack went and paid for the ice hut. He decided to take it to his truck and not have to worry about it later. Surprised to see the snow he opened up his tail gate and slid the box in. Then he closed it, all the while thinking with this kind of weather the state park is going to look beautiful. This was the first snowfall of the year. The pine and spruce trees will look spectacular with the snow covering their branches and the layer of snow covering the ground will keep the creatures warm beneath the surface. Nature had a way of protecting its own. On his way back in he passed Maggie, not realizing she was even there. He was still thinking about the winter wonderland he would be going home to.

"Hi, Jack," said Maggie, "nice buy."

"Oh, Maggie, thanks, I thought so too," he said startled. "I was just lucky Dale didn't bid more."

Stew had entered the auction room and saw Maggie and Jack talking. There was a lull in the auctioneer's voice and a hum from the crowd talking. The auctioneer was taking a break before the next big item. Maggie was telling Jack she heard that the local Soul River Marina, owned and operated by Kent Newsley had donated a snowmobile. Big items like this are not often submitted, but the word is that Mr. Newsley likes Mrs. Murphy and wanted to do something nice for her and the church. Jack was very impressed but the state supplied snowmobiles for park rangers so they could do their jobs in the parks during the winter season. He didn't need to bid on this one, but what a great buy it would be for someone.

"Hi, Maggie," said Stew, giving her a hug and a kiss on the cheek in front of Jack.

"Hi, Stew," said Maggie returning the hug.

"Jack, this is Stew, he's a teacher in Hainesley and Stew, this is Jack, he's a park ranger at the Carleton Falls State Park."

The guys exchanged handshakes, and pleasantries. Stew said he had to go and pick up Emma from work and may be back later. He asked if they would be here for a while. Maggie said she was staying and would like to see Emma. Stew said they would be back if Emma wasn't too tired. Jack said he was staying for a while as well. Stew said his goodbyes and told Jack it was nice meeting him.

"Who is Emma?" asked Jack.

"Oh, Emma is Stew's fiancé, they're getting married on New Year's Eve. Stew has asked me to make their wedding cake and the desserts for the reception."

"That's great, Maggie," said Jack, quite enthused at the two of them getting married.

Now he could ask Maggie out knowing she didn't have a boyfriend. Maggie could feel Jack was happier and less standoffish. What was going on with him? She didn't have the patience to find out and figured she would just ask him.

"Jack, what's going on with you? One time we're enjoying each other's company. The next time you're very distant and tonight you were just making conversation and now you're happier than a lark. Would you care to explain?"

Hearing it like that, he felt rather ridiculous. He wasn't aware how Maggie saw things. There was never a girl that made him act this way or feel this way, until Maggie. He wanted to date her so they could become good friends. He really liked Maggie and wanted to see how a relationship would work out. This was a wakeup call for Jack, and Maggie was the one waking him up.

"I should be honest with you, Maggie. The day I saw you and Jasper in front of Town Hardware, I was inside buying an ice fishing rod and reel for you. I wanted to ask you out on a date. Then I saw you hugging and kissing Stew. I thought you and Stew had gotten together and I was too late. I was upset with myself because I hadn't called you sooner."

Maggie looking wide eyed at Jack couldn't believe just how upset Jack had been that day. He must really like her, she thought.

"So why didn't you call me Jack, it only takes one call."

"I didn't call you because I was dealing with my mother's illness. She had severe pneumonia and had to be hospitalized. At one point they didn't think she was going to make it. I had taken a leave of absence and went to Canada to be with her. Her sister had passed on two years ago, so it's just her and me. I had to keep focused on her and I didn't need any distractions. Not that you're a distraction in a bad way but you would have been a beautiful distraction for sure."

"I understand Jack. It was the same with my dad. It takes strength to keep focused. You tell yourself that you need to be strong for them, all the while we need someone to be strong for us too. A shoulder we can lean on. How is your mother now?"

"She came through it just fine. I realized I wanted to be closer to her and moved her to a small apartment in Hainesley. I visit as often as I can and she loves it. She has been getting acquainted with some of the other renters and slowly starting a new life for herself. She would like you Maggie, and you her. In some ways you're alike, especially your strengths."

"I'm glad she's okay. I would love to meet her some time. She sounds like a wonderful person."

"Oh, she is. There is one more thing, since I'm being so open with you. I told you why I didn't get in touch with you but I didn't tell you why I wanted to ask you out on a date."

Jack stopped talking and brought Maggie closer to him. He placed one hand gently behind her neck and the other hand on her waist. He looked into her beautiful green eyes as her soft blonde curls framed her face. Her lips were a luscious deep red and her smile so infectious. Her pants were hugging her in all the right places and the soft sweater she was wearing caressed her breasts, which also made her figure so enticing.

"Almost losing my mother I realized that someday I would be alone. I didn't like the feeling and if I could have anyone in my life, who would that one person be? It's you Maggie; I think we would make a great couple and I ..."

He leaned in to give her a kiss. Maggie didn't resist and it was exciting yet comforting at the same time. The softness of his lips on hers was quite inviting. His muscular arms gently around her and him pulling her closely to his chest gave her a state of calmness. All the stress had left her body. This feeling she had long-awaited for, a feeling of home, a feeling of being safe, and most of all loved.

"Wow, ah . . . yes, I will go out with you Jack," said Maggie stunned and her breath taken away by Jack's kiss.

Jack very happy held Maggie's hand, not wanting to let her go. All her friends were right, Maggie thought. They all saw it in Jack's eyes and hers that night at the Halloween dance.

The auction went very well and it was Dale that bought the snowmobile. When he talked to Jack about it, he said that he needed to buy a new one. The snow can get pretty deep at the park. Dale and Kim needed another way to get into town if their truck couldn't make it. The bid stopped at $10,500. Dale had been pricing them and even at $10,500 it was a very good deal. He priced it at $16,900 at the Marina. So, it was well worth it for sure. Dale must have been sure he was going home with it because he brought his trailer.

Jack gave Dale a hand putting the snowmobile in his trailer and Maggie went to the auditorium. The music was quite loud and a lot of people were on the dance floor. She saw Kim and went over to talk to her. Kim was excited for her and Jack. She could see that Maggie was glowing and so happy. The only advice she could give Maggie was to fully enjoy each other's company when they were together. Maggie said she intended to do just that. Kim was also happy that Dale had the winning bid for the snowmobile. It was something she was happy to have around in case of an emergency at the store during the snowy weather.

Julie and her husband Will had finished a dance and came to talk to Maggie and Kim. Julie knew something was up by the look on Maggie's face. When she told them about Jack, they were both happy for her. Maggie could use a shoulder to lean on once in a while, Julie thought. Ella and Liz were also in the crowd. Ella waved as she was dancing with Mark. There dating was still going strong and they made a wonderful couple. Liz and Anna had come together. Anna's husband was in bed with a cold, so they decided to team up and take one car. Anna showed Maggie the bracelet she bid on when the auction first started. It only cost her $25.00. It was a beautiful sterling silver charm bracelet with one heart charm on it. She was so excited.

The food and desserts had almost sold out. This fundraiser was turning out to be the best one ever.

Maggie could see Mrs. Murphy from across the room. She looked so happy and was talking to Kent Newsley. Maggie hoped that one day they would get together.

"May I have this dance?" Jack said, finally finding Maggie in the auditorium.

"Of course, Jack," said Maggie.

Jack escorted Maggie to the dance floor, holding her hand. The music was slow and Jack brought Maggie close to him with his arms around her waist. Maggie placed her arms on Jack's shoulders. Their bodies moved to the rhythm of the music. They might as well have been the only ones on the dance floor. The other couples stopped to watch them dance. Pretty much everyone at the fundraiser knew Maggie. They were all happy to see her with someone. She was always there to help out others and she deserved to have someone in her life that cared for her. The tempo of the music changed as Jack and Maggie moved quickly to the beat of the song while still looking attentively into each other's eyes. They were definitely the attraction of the night.

It was getting late and the majority of people had already left. Maggie and Jack saw Mrs. Murphy and mentioned what a great time they both had. Mrs. Murphy thanked them for coming and said it was nice to see them together. Again Mrs. Murphy was right, Maggie thought. Jack asked if he could drive Maggie home but Maggie having left her car at the bakery, asked him to drop her off there. They walked to the exit door and when they opened it, they both looked at each other. The amount of snow that had fallen was a good foot. No snow plows had been out as most of the town was at the fundraiser.

"Why don't we walk to the bakery and wait until the roads are clear," said Maggie.

"Great idea, why get stuck if we have a place to stay."

CHAPTER 22

"Time to get up, you two. It's a brand-new day," Julie chuckled as she woke Jack and Maggie up from their sleep. "Business as usual, we have a lot to get done."

Maggie still had her outfit on from last night and so did Jack. They had curled up on the cot that Maggie had in the back room. She had it in there just in case she ever had to stay over. Julie brought them both a coffee. They looked like they needed it. Jack used the washroom first as he needed to splash his face with cold water to wake up. Maggie told him she had extra toothbrushes in the cabinet drawer. She liked to buy three or four of them when they are on sale. He sat at the table where the girls usually ate their lunch taking large sips of his coffee. Julie heated up a couple of scones for Jack and put them on a plate in front of him with butter and honey.

"Thanks, Julie, what a nice surprise."

"You're welcome, it was Maggie's idea."

While Jack was eating Maggie was getting changed. She put on a pair of jeans and a sweater from the closet beside the cot. These were her change into clothes for the bakery. Maggie called Charlie to let him know she stayed at the bakery all night because of the weather and asked if he was taking Jasper to Flora's house. He said he had talked to her and she was going to come to his place this time. She said it gets her and Tilly out and the roads were good for driving, as the snowplows had been out early this morning. Julie had reminded her that Noah would be here any minute to start working. Just then Ella came back to let Julie know that Noah was in fact out front. She was surprised to see Jack and said good morning to him, putting two and two together.

"Ella, just tell Noah to come back and we'll get started," said Julie.

"Good morning, Noah, this is Jack, Maggie will be with you in a moment."

"Nice to meet you, Jack," said Noah as he shook Jack's hand.

"Nice to meet you too," said Jack looking at Noah and wondering why Maggie is hiring someone that should be on the cover of a magazine. He just started dating Maggie. Did he have to worry about Noah stealing her away from him?

"Hi, Noah, glad you're here. The sink is over there to wash your hands and here is a clean apron and hair net. I would like you to make apple strudel this morning, just one, cut into eight even pieces. The dough is already prepared, and in the walk-in. If you need to know anything else, just ask Julie."

"Thanks, Maggie, I'll get right on it."

"Now, as for you mister, did you enjoy your scones and coffee," said Maggie looking into Jack's eyes.

"Yes, very much," said Jack. "I don't usually have such a nice breakfast. Thank you. What do you say about going skating with me tonight? You do know how to skate, don't you?"

"Yes, I do, and I would love to go skating with you."

"Great, I will pick you up around six and we will eat first then go skating, but I will need your address, Maggie."

"It's 34 Meadow Street, would you like directions, Jack."

"No, I'll find it. See you tonight, Maggie," said Jack as he again leaned in to give her a kiss.

Both Julie and Noah saw them kissing. Was Jack staking his claim on Maggie, showing Noah, she was his? One thing was for sure; Jack was falling in love with Maggie and didn't want to lose her. Jack said goodbye and went to get his truck over at the church. Today being Saturday, he had a lot of errands to do before getting back to the state park.

Noah had finished the strudel and asked Maggie to take a look at it. Julie had mentioned to him that they do the puff pastry into a rectangle with the filling down the middle. Both sides cut into one-inch strips then crisscrossed over the filling, from side to side. Not all bakers arranged their strudel pastry the same way but Maggie preferred it like this. It took a bit longer but for the look that Maggie wanted, it was well worth it.

"It looks perfect, Noah, well done," said Maggie. "I'm turning you over to Julie. She has orders to get ready and we need day to day baking for out front. Just follow her instructions. The girls usually let her know when they're running short. We also bake backups and keep them in the walk-in for the next day. You'll do fine."

Noah smiled, so pleased that he would fit in okay with his new co-workers. He knew he would love to work at Magpie Bakery, it reminded him of his mom's bakery, something he had really missed.

Maggie now had time to work on her grandmother's coffee for the shop but first things first. She called Charlie to let him know she would be home later this afternoon to get Jasper. He said Jasper was having a great time especially with the snow outside. They had already gone for three walks this morning.

"Jasper sure gets you doing things that you normally wouldn't do. I may have to reconsider getting a dog of my own," laughed Charlie. "Flora and Tilly are here now and Tilly is loving it too. Flora said she couldn't be happier about the progress Tilly has made."

"That's great Charlie, I'm glad you're enjoying all the company. I have a dinner date tonight and will have to leave Jasper at home," said Maggie a little apprehensive to ask Charlie to watch Jasper again.

"Wonderful, Maggie, you deserve to have fun, you work so hard. I will keep Jasper another day. It's all settled, I don't want to hear another word about it."

"Thanks, Charlie, I will drop off some more food for Jasper when I come home to change and don't bother making supper tonight for yourself. You deserve a Shepherd's pie and a cherry pie for dessert."

"Yes, I have been working hard all day," he said jokingly while laughing. "Thank you, Maggie I will look forward to it."

"Maybe you might want to invite a dinner guest as well. Bye, Charlie, see you later."

Maggie went to the back storage room. Where did I put them? she wondered, as she went through some boxes. Jasper Cookie bags, more cookie bags, ah . . . there they are. They were folded boxes with an inner plastic liner to keep the coffee fresh. After all, the box would be opened and closed quite a few times getting the product out. The company also put Maggie's logo on the front of the box, Magpie Bakery. But the name was the biggest thrill for Maggie, Alice's Coffee written under the logo right across the front in big bold fancy letters. Her grandmother would have been so proud of Maggie and happy to know something she had done was now something everyone could have. Back then it was just a recipe but now seeing people coming from far away to try her coffee, it was remarkable. If only I could go back in time and help her start her own business, Maggie thought, she might have had a better life. But then her grandmother was always happy and upbeat. She was a very positive person, always helping others, that's what made her truly happy, helping others. It gave her a purpose in life, something some people strive for their whole life and never find. Maggie needed to stay focused if she was going to get some on the shelf today for the customers to buy. The coffee had to be weighed and packaged properly. She made a dozen, priced them and put them on the shelf out front. She put a couple on top of the showcase as well. Eventually the word would get around she thought.

"Hi, Maggie," said a familiar voice.

"Good morning, Jane, how are you?"

"I'm good, everything is great. Business is really good; people are buying for Christmas. I really can't complain. I see you're quite busy too."

"Yes," said Maggie, "people coming in and buying my plum pudding pies early and freezing them. Any pie really doesn't sit on the shelf. They want to make sure they have one for Christmas. Plus having a drive-thru has added a great increase in traffic flow for sure."

Pies, Maggie thought, I better grab a cherry pie for Charlie. She didn't know if there were more in the walk-in.

"Excuse me Jane, I just need to get a cherry pie for Charlie."

Maggie quickly grabbed a cherry pie off the shelf and went back to Jane's table. Only one left she told Jane and thank goodness because she didn't want to disappoint Charlie.

Jane smiled and nodded her head. Jane liked Charlie as well. Jane's father Edward was a good friend of Charlie's while Jane was growing up. They were both into computer software and technology. When Charlie became CEO of a company, he knew Edward would be a great benefit to the company.

Edward was grateful to Charlie for helping him and his family. Their relationship grew from there. Jane's mother would ask Charlie for supper at least once a week so they could catch up on things. Even though they worked for the same company, they rarely saw each other during office hours. Then years later when her father was ready to retire and enjoy life with the family, Edward had a car accident. He stayed late that night to finish up on paperwork so the new employee would have a less stressful beginning to their new job. It was very cold out that night and it had been snowing. Edward had traveled these roads for years but the temperature was even colder than he anticipated. Had he left at his usual time, it might not have been so icy. His car slid and he crashed into a guard rail. He made it out alive but he had endured a severe brain injury. Since the accident he has been a resident of the Hainesley Unity Nursing Home. Charlie goes to visit him once a week. Even though Edward doesn't know who anyone is, Charlie goes out of respect for Jane and her parents. But Jane thinks it's more than that. She went to visit one day and she heard Charlie in the room talking. She looked in to see and it was Charlie reading a book to her father and her father staring into the room with a smile on his face. It was like he could understand what Charlie was reading or maybe it was the soothing tone of Charlie's voice. It really didn't matter. What mattered was that they still enjoyed each other's company. It meant a lot to Jane and her mother too.

"I should be going; the jewellery store isn't going to run itself. I put a note on the door saying when I would be back. Nice to see you Maggie, say hi to Charlie for me."

"Bye Jane, I'll see you at the Christmas tree lighting, if not sooner."

"Yes. I'll be there, take care."

Maggie took Charlie's pie to the walk-in and let Julie and Noah know that it was taken and not to put it out front. Julie said Noah was doing a great job; it was like he had been working here for years. Noah told Maggie he had been in contact with Bill Rowen and is going to look at a house apartment after work. If everything works out okay, he might be a new resident of Carleton Falls. Maggie was happy to hear that. Noah was just the person she needed as another baker. Living in Carleton Falls meant he was here to stay.

Maggie started peeling potatoes and had the ground beef cooking on the stove. Liz came back to let Maggie know she had sold one of her boxed coffees. Maggie thanked her for letting her know. It certainly put an instant smile on Maggie's face.

"Has everyone had their lunch, Liz?"

"Yes, we all took turns," said Liz.

"Good, said Maggie. You all know if you need me to fill in out front to just come and get me, right?"

"We know, Maggie, we're good," said Liz as she was walking away from Maggie and heading back to the front.

Maggie drained the potatoes and whipped them up with a little milk and butter. She added a little beef gravy to the meat and some frozen vegetables as well and let it simmer while she went to get a deep-dish pie plate. The aroma was making Maggie hungry. She took a spoon from the drawer and a small bowl from the shelf. She added some of the meat mixture and topped it off with a spoonful of whipped potatoes. She couldn't resist … mmm … Charlie is really going to enjoy this, she thought. Once she finished, she added the meat mixture to the pie plate. The whipped potatoes went on next covering the meat below. Under the broiler for a few minutes to brown the potatoes and it was ready to go. Maggie turned off the oven and put it on a cooling rack. She wrapped it up with foil then she went to put a few Jasper cookies in the walk-in next to the cherry pie. She didn't want to forget a treat for Jasper and maybe even Tilly.

Maggie got all her clothes together and told Julie she was heading out. She asked Julie how it looked for tomorrow with the baked goods. Julie said that they were way ahead thanks to Noah and tomorrow should be quite busy after church is over. Maggie agreed and said her goodbyes. She went to get Charlie's food and went out the back door to her car. She couldn't wait to get home and have a shower. Maggie drove up to Charlie's house and took him the pies and cookies. He was so happy and so was Jasper to see Maggie. Flora was still there with Tilly and Charlie had asked her to stay for supper. Flora was quite happy to stay and was enjoying herself spending time with Charlie. He loved to play chess and Flora was top player in her chess club at school, back in the day. Charlie couldn't be happier that he found a chess buddy. Maggie had a couple of hours before Jack was going to pick her up. She told Charlie and Flora she would take Jasper home for a while and bring him back in an hour and a half. She would also bring some kibble when she came back for Jasper and Tilly. Charlie knew Maggie wanted to spend some time with Jasper and said he will see her then.

Jasper was happy to be home. The first thing he found was his chew rope, his favourite toy. Maggie ran down to the basement looking for her skates. She hadn't worn them in years and hoped they were sharp enough. They were hanging by their laces on a nail that was partially nailed into the rafters. They would have to do she thought as she ran back upstairs. Jasper was still contently playing with his chew rope. Maggie put fresh water into his water bowl and poured kibble into his dish. She went to her closet and took out a black pair of jeans and a cream-coloured turtleneck sweater. She laid them out on her bed; next she retrieved her ski jacket and knee-high boots. Mitts, hat and a scarf were in order too. Now it was time to take a shower.

CHAPTER 23

Maggie had just stepped out of the shower, and heard someone knocking at the front door and Jasper barking. Who could it be she wondered, maybe Charlie needing something or Flora. She grabbed a towel quickly and put it around her. As she opened the door slightly to see who it was Jasper had nudged between her and the door, pushing it wide open. Standing on the other side was Jack.

"Jack, you're early."

"No, I'm pretty sure I said I would pick you up around six. If anything, I'm a few minutes late. Aren't you cold, Maggie?"

"Yes of course, come in please. Jasper, come here, boy."

Maggie looked at the clock on the wall. It was after six and now she had to hurry and get ready. She must have thought it was four o'clock when she left work and it was closer to five.

"I'm sorry, Jack, I lost track of time."

"Jack approached Maggie and placed his hands around her face then gave her a kiss on the forehead. I kind of like your towel outfit. It looks quite becoming on you."

"Thanks, Jack, why don't you and Jasper get reacquainted and I will be as quick as I can," said Maggie feeling a little flustered.

She put on her clothes and decided the night called for a little perfume. Something she never wore except for special occasions. She suddenly thought she might be wearing it a little more often. She put some blush on her cheeks and used a little bronzer. Lip stick would not be needed tonight, just a little lip gloss instead. Her hair was dry and all she had to do was fix her curls. She could hear Jack talking to Jasper and playing with him. She hoped he was okay with her being late. She felt so bad, what if he had made reservations she thought, we would be late. Not a good way to start off dating.

"Okay, I'm ready," she said with her coat and skates in hand. "Do I look all right?"

"Well, I prefer the towel look better, but this is a close second."

Maggie smiled. "We should get going, I've held up things long enough."

Maggie filled a bag with some kibble for Jasper and Tilly. Jack helped Maggie with her coat and carried her skates.

"The man across the street is going to watch Jasper for me. I would like you to meet him," said Maggie as she locked the front door.

Maggie rang the doorbell as Jasper was eager to get inside. Charlie opened the door and Jasper ran in.

"Come in, Maggie, I see you have someone with you."

"Yes, Charlie, this is Jack Kincaid and Jack, this is Charlie MacEwan."

Both men shook hands and said how nice it was to meet each other. Charlie introduced Flora to Jack as well. Maggie gave some kibble to Jasper and Tilly while the guys were in conversation. Even Flora and Tilly were brought into the discussion. Charlie and Flora thanked Maggie for supper. He mentioned how tasty the Shepherd's pie was, as always and how much they both enjoyed it. Flora was getting quite tired and decided to leave with Tilly saying good night to all of them, having had a very enjoyable day. Maggie thanked Charlie again for watching Jasper and keeping him over night and left extra kibble for Jasper as well. She asked both Charlie and Jack if they would be interested in making cookies with her at the bakery Monday night. Charlie was a definite yes and Jack was a little hesitant and surprised, but agreed to help them. Jack told Charlie it was nice meeting him and he couldn't wait for cookie day. Charlie laughed and then said good night to Maggie.

Maggie didn't know where Jack was taking her. His truck was certainly ready for winter. Maggie couldn't help but notice he had all terrain tires on the vehicle. After twenty minutes of driving, she decided to ask him where they were going.

"Well, I figured there was no better place to skate than at Carleton Falls State Park and no better place to eat than Jack's place."

Maggie looked at Jack and chuckled. "So, you cook too?" asked Maggie.

"Yes, I have been known to cook a mean beans and wieners."

"You have," laughed Maggie, "and is that on the menu tonight?"

"Oh, something even more special than beans and wieners. It's in the warming tray as we speak. Already cooked and ready to eat when we get there."

"I can't wait, I am getting hungry."

"It won't be much longer," Jack said, touching her hand.

It started snowing and Jack turned on the windshield wipers to see the road. There were no other cars on the road and very quiet. The snow was falling slowly to the ground in a peaceful manner covering up their tracks as they made their way to the state park.

"I think we are on the road that took me to my campsite."

"Yes, you're right, we need to stay on this then make a right when we get to a division in the road," Jack said, as he looked at Maggie wondering where he was taking her.

Maggie was trying to remember every turn that Jack took. Up ahead she saw a cabin with smoke coming out of the chimney. It was a beautiful sight with trees all around it and with the snow falling; made it even prettier. Down the river a bit she could see lights and people skating. Jack pulled up at the back of the cabin then turned around and backed in. Once he turned off the truck he came around and opened Maggie's door. He held her hand as she got out of the truck and still holding onto it, he opened the cabin door. Once inside Maggie thought it was beautiful, her dad would have loved it. The stone fireplace was floor to ceiling and in the center of the cabin. It was a double-sided fireplace. In front was a comfy looking beige couch and two dark-brown leather recliners on either side of the fireplace. The floors were wide-plank pine. It was obvious they were original to the cabin. Under the furniture was a beautiful earth-tone area rug with beiges, browns and greens beautifully displayed throughout the carpet. On the other side of the fireplace was the kitchen and dining room. The kitchen cupboards were also made of pine. They had been well taken care of and Jack had the dining room table all set up with candles at either end. It was very impressive, especially for a man living alone. On the left side of the cabin past the living room were two bedrooms and a bathroom. The fireplace could literally heat the whole place. It was so cozy and warm. Viewing the fire from the living room on one side and the kitchen and dining room on the other side was so comforting. Why would anyone ever want to leave? thought Maggie as she took off her boots. Jack removing his noticed the intrigue in Maggie's face.

"Why did you have a campsite, Jack, when you have this beautiful cabin?"

"I love to sleep under the stars whenever I can. It just brings me closer to nature and reminds me of camping with my family. I'm fortunate that I can have both. Why don't you sit down at the dining room table and I will get us a glass of wine," said Jack as he headed to the kitchen counter.

Maggie made herself comfortable as Jack placed a glass of wine in her hand. The aroma of the food filled the whole cabin. She couldn't wait to see what it was. She took a sip of her wine. It was a medium-bodied red wine, very nice and smooth.

"Your meal will be served in just a moment," he said as he went to dish it out.

Jack placed a plate in front of Maggie and a plate for himself. It was a fair-sized slice of lasagna with a side of garlic bread and a fresh salad. Maggie tried the lasagna and Jack was waiting to see if she liked it.

"Did you make this yourself, Jack? It's delicious."

"I just followed my mother's recipe. It's pretty fail-safe."

"You can cook for me anytime, Jack, so much for beans and wieners. This is an outstanding meal."

"I'm glad you like it," said Jack. "I'm not quite as good making desserts though. I made something simple, again my mother's idea."

Once they had finished the main meal, Jack brought out dessert. He had made a chocolate pudding topped with whipped cream and a glazed cherry. Whether it tasted good or not he got top marks for display. It looked incredible. Maggie took a spoonful and closed her eyes.

"There is something other than chocolate in this pudding," she said to Jack. "I'm not quite sure what it is though."

"Yes, it's my mother's secret ingredient," Jack laughed.

"Really," said Maggie.

"No," said Jack, "it's half butterscotch and chocolate mixed."

"Well, you had me fooled it's very delicious. The whole meal was great."

Maggie and Jack did the dishes together, while stopping in between to have a sip of wine. Jack noticed the fire was getting low and said he needed to split a few logs for overnight. Maggie said she would finish up and he could tend to the wood. Jack put on his boots and went outside.

Maggie wondered why he didn't take his coat. The snow was still coming down gently, sparkling as it hit the ice filled river. Watching Jack from a kitchen window, Maggie now knew why he was so muscular. It was from splitting wood. Each time he grabbed the axe in his hands and lifted it up in the air you could see his muscles bulge, then whack, the axe was forced right into the wood, splitting it in two. His arms and chest were getting a real work out. Maggie could see he was working up a sweat, even without his coat on. It only took him a short while, as long as it took her to finish cleaning up. Through the back door he came with an armful of wood. He threw some into the fire and stacked the rest in a metal box next to the fireplace. He then went back out to get some more and did this, three more times. On his last trip he asked her if she was ready to go skating.

Maggie bundled herself up with her ski jacket, hat, scar and mitts. Her knee-high boots were next. Jack grabbed his coat and a toque and put on his boots. He carried their skates in one hand and held her hand in the other. Down to the skating rink they went. There were people and kids everywhere, enjoying the outdoors. There was music and a man selling hot chocolate. There were benches all around the rink for those that got tired and wanted to sit and watch. Maggie slipped off her boots and put her skates on. Jack did the same. He took her hand and escorted her to the ice rink.

"Ready," he said, as he held her one hand and then put his other hand around Maggie's waist to steady her.

Maggie looked up at him and nodded. Off they went, just as graceful as if they were dancing. They both surprised each other. Skating must be like riding a bike. Once you learn you never forget how, Maggie thought. It had been a good five to six years since she was on skates, she even impressed herself.

Jack was great on skates, a natural. The outdoors just suited him, it was definitely in his blood. He said as a kid growing up in Canada, he used to play on a hockey team. He really enjoyed it until he had a serious sprain. It took a long time to heal and a few physiotherapists later.

They were both having a great time and even enjoyed a cup of hot chocolate. They skated a few more rounds and then decided to head back to the cabin. The snow was coming down a little quicker now. It was so pretty Maggie thought. As she was looking up at the falling snow she tripped and fell into a snow bank. Jack picked her up and asked her if she was all right. Maggie let him know she was okay but really didn't want him to let her go. She looked into his eyes and he placed a kiss on her lips. "Let's get you back to the cabin so you can warm up in front of the fire and we can have another glass of wine," said Jack, still holding on to Maggie.

Jack opened the door and Maggie stepped in. The warmth of the fireplace engulfed her entire body. The chill in her bones had quickly disappeared. She took a seat on the couch in front of the fire and Jack sat beside her. They each had a glass of wine and were talking about their childhood and how they grew up. Jack had his arm around Maggie's shoulder and contently listened as she was talking about her dad. Jack could see why she looked up to her father so much. She talked about the silly things he used to do to make her laugh. Her laugh was infectious and as he sat there gazing into her green eyes, he felt like he could see within her soul. It was at that very moment he knew he was in love with Maggie. There would be no other. He suddenly realized that he didn't want to spend the rest of his life without her. But did she feel the same way, he wondered? The way she was when they first met told him that she wasn't interested in having a man around. Was it just two people enjoying each other's company or was it more?

They spent hours talking and Jack got up to put some music on and asked Maggie for a dance. The music was slow tempo with a variation of string instruments. He wrapped his arms around Maggie not wanting to ever let her go. Maggie placed her head on his chest listening to the pulsating beat of his heart. It was like it was keeping time with the music. She felt secure with Jack's arms around her and could stay like that all night long. Dance after dance they held on tightly to each other as time swept by.

Once the music stopped, they both noticed it was getting cooler in the cabin. Jack put more wood on top of the burning embers in the fireplace. Maggie looked out the windows to a blanket of snow blowing in the direction of the river. The snow was coming down so thick she couldn't even see Jack's truck. They had been enjoying the night cozy and warm so much that they forgot to keep an eye on the weather.

"Jack, there's a storm out there. I can't even see your truck."

"All roads are closed in and out of the park," Jack said, as he looked up the Carleton Falls State Park weather advisory on his cell phone.

"I guess we are here for the night, Maggie. Maybe you should call Charlie and let him know."

"Yes, good idea, I wouldn't want him to worry. I hope he hasn't gone to bed early. Hi, Charlie, I didn't want you to worry but Jack and I are here at his cabin at the state park. There is a bad snowstorm and all roads are closed. Is it snowing there?"

"We're fine, Maggie. It is snowing but only an inch or two on the ground so far. When you do come home tomorrow you and Jack take your time and be safe. Whenever you get home Jasper and I will be here, day or night."

"Thanks, Charlie, you're the best. Would you call Flora and let her know, please? See you sometime tomorrow and give Jasper a hug for me, good night."

"Night, Maggie, I will let Flora know, see you tomorrow."

Maggie felt more at ease now having called Charlie. She knew they were safe and could take her time tomorrow picking Jasper up.

"Would you like another glass of wine, Maggie?" asked Jack. "We don't have to worry about driving anywhere."

"Yes please, I really don't know when I've had a more enjoyable evening. Everything has been perfect, Jack. You are quite the guy."

Jack smiled as he poured some wine into Maggie's glass and then into his as he joined her on the couch.

"I'm glad you think so. I think you're quite the woman."

Maggie returned a smile as they both leaned in for a kiss. This time it was a very passionate kiss.

"Oh no, I'm sorry, Jack," Maggie said as she picked up the wineglass off her lap.

"That's all right the couch can be cleaned, and most of it went on you anyway," said Jack thinking she really is accident-prone. "Why don't you take a quick shower and I will find you something of mine to put on."

"Yes, it went through my sweater. I am feeling a little sticky."

Jack found Maggie a long T-shirt to wear and a pair of pajama bottoms as well. They would be big on her but she could always roll them up, he thought. He didn't want to go into the bathroom and leave them while she was in the shower. He figured it would be better if he waited until she asked for them. While she was in the shower Jack took a cloth from under the sink and wet it. He then sprayed a fabric cleaner on it and took both the cleaner and cloth to the couch. He rubbed the cloth on the wine stain. He didn't need to apply a lot of pressure the stain was coming out nicely. He turned the cloth over and sprayed on more fabric cleaner. With another rub the stain was completely gone, just a damp spot in its place.

The bathroom door opened and Maggie was standing in the doorway with a towel wrapped around her.

"Did you find any clothes for me, Jack?"

Jack brought the clothes to Maggie, and looked into her eyes.

"I still like the towel look better, Maggie."

Maggie grabbed Jacks arm and pulled him into the bathroom, closing the door behind him.

CHAPTER 24

Jack got up early to make Maggie breakfast. He opened the back door to see how it looked outside. The snow had drifted halfway up the door. He had a broom against the wall in the kitchen and used it to sweep the snow off and away from the door. The storm was over and it was a clear sunny new day. He smiled to himself thinking it was a great new day, a new beginning for sure. He then carried on with breakfast and put the coffee on. He put some bacon into the oven along with two sausage patties. He then mixed the eggs and poured them into a pan on low. As he poured two cups of coffee, he realized he didn't know what Maggie took in her coffee.

"Anyway, is fine with me Jack," said Maggie as she saw Jack looking perplexed. "It smells wonderful. Is the storm over?"

"It looks like it, I haven't looked to see if the roads are open yet," Jack said as he looked at Maggie standing there in his T-shirt.

"Here you go; scrambled eggs, sausage, bacon and toast. Here is some of my mother's homemade jam, if you would like some. Take a seat and enjoy."

"It looks great," she said as she tried the eggs. "It tastes great too. You out did yourself again. I could get use to this," she chuckled.

Jack smiled at Maggie then took a mouthful of his scrambled eggs and went to put more wood on the fire. He then looked at his phone for the weather details, Maggie looking at every move Jack made, not wanting to take her eyes off of him.

"The roads are open," he said, "but I have a better idea."

"And what would that be?"

"I would like to take you ice fishing; we can even try out my new ice hut."

Maggie didn't want to answer right away until she thought it over. There was Jasper to think about and her bakery. First, Charlie said to pick up Jasper, day or night so she didn't have to bother rushing home. Second, she had a great bunch of employees and they could run the shop for one day. She would call to let them know what was going on.

"Yes, Jack, it's a great idea."

"Perfect," he said as giddy as a little boy.

Maggie could see the kid coming out in him. It was nice seeing him happy after everything he had dealt with regarding his mother's illness.

"What do you suggest I wear, Jack?" said Maggie as her clothes were still stained with wine.

She had left them in a pail to soak overnight and planned to wash them in the morning. Jack had a small apartment size washer and dryer, so it wouldn't be a problem.

"Well, I have more towels," said Jack jokingly. I think a pair of jogging pants with the legs gathered would fit you better for length, they won't go passed your ankles and you can roll up the waist. But I think it's your decision. You help yourself to anything of mine that you need, including the extra toothbrush under the sink in the bathroom."

"Thank you, I'm sure I will find something."

Maggie and Jack talked about ice fishing while finishing their breakfast. Maggie could get used to seeing Jack sitting across from her every morning. Was she falling in love with Jack? Was this what being in love felt like? she wondered. She was happy and Jack made her happy. He made her feel secure, relaxed, safe and most of all loved. He felt like home. That same feeling she had, being with her dad. The only other person that ever gave her that feeling was Charlie.

"More bacon, Maggie, or coffee?"

"Yes, both please," said Maggie as she picked up her phone. "Thank you, I'm just going to call the bakery and let Julie know my plans for today."

As she started to dial, she watched Jack clear the table. Nice to see a man who takes charge and sees what needs to be done and does it. Her dad used to be the same way but not her uncle William, her dad's brother. They were two totally different people. William was dependent on everyone including his wife, Eleanor. It used to bother her that she was left to do dishes or clean up. But she said it took so much energy to get him to help, that it was just quicker to do it herself. Maggie remembered her dad saying, about that subject, that your uncle William was a lot smarter than people gave him credit. I guess it got him out of doing a lot of things, but he missed out on doing them with someone he loved. To this day she still waits on him, and wouldn't have it any other way.

"Hi, Julie, I won't be coming in today. Will you be able to handle the day with Noah's help?"

"Yes, Maggie, we'll be fine. Noah wants me to let you know he found a place to rent and is moving his belongings tonight. He has a few friends to help him so it shouldn't take too long."

"That's great, I'm happy for him. It is a long commute when the roads are snow covered. He won't have to get up as early to get to work. Does he need any help, Julie?"

"No, he says he's good and says thank you for the offer. Are you not feeling well, Maggie?"

"As a matter of fact, I feel great," said Maggie as she looked at Jack. "Jack has asked me to go ice fishing today, so I thought I would take the day off."

"Oh, Jack is it," Julie laughed. "Good for you, have fun and tell Jack hi."

"Thanks, I will," said Maggie as she ended the call.

"Julie says hi and they will be fine at the bakery. Noah found a rental and is moving tonight."

"Do you think he could use any help?" Jack asked, as he scrubbed the last plate.

"I asked Julie the same thing. He said he was good and said thank you for asking."

Maggie got up from the table and took a dish towel to dry the plates. Jack finished at the sink, dried his hands and put them around Maggie's waist drawing her in closer. He gave her a little peck on the cheek teasing her as she looked into his eyes.

He smiled and gave her a long intense kiss. Something he had wanted to do all morning.

"I'll finish up and put the dishes away if you want to get dressed and get the gear ready," said Maggie.

"Sounds good, it might take me a while. I'm going to take a quick shower first."

Maggie could hear the shower running and went to get a towel from the hall closet. She thought he might need one since she had used the two towels that were in the bathroom and put them all in the laundry basket. She knocked at the door then went in.

"Jack, I used all the towels, I thought you might need one. I'll leave it for you."

Jack opened the shower door and invited her in. Maggie removed his T-shirt and joined him, feeling the warmth of the water trickling down her body. Jack told her it was a good way of saving water.

"I'll be back in about an hour. It will take time to get the ice hut set up and gear ready. I'll add wood to the fireplace before I leave, so you'll be warm. Then I'll come back to get you when everything is ready," said Jack as he gave Maggie another kiss and hug, then handed her a towel. "Maggie, I think I've found a new look I like," he said as he walked out the door.

Maggie knew that Jack was the guy for her. She wanted to be with him every second. Even now, knowing he would be back she wanted to be with him. She wondered if he felt the same way. Should she ask him or wait and hope he says something? Maggie wasn't sure what to do. She went into Jack's bedroom and looked through his closet to find something to wear. She found a black pair of jogging pants like he had mentioned. It did make sense to wear something that was warm and the bottom of the legs were gathered. Maggie stepped into the pants and pulled them up. Not bad she thought even if they were on the big side. She rolled the band and they seemed to fit a bit better, now for a shirt. His sweat shirt was quite warm but too bulky and big to wear under her ski jacket. She decided to put on a short sleeve T-shirt, then over it, a long sleeve T-shirt that was a little heavier. She then tucked everything into the sweat pants and added a pair of his socks to her ensemble. Jack's socks were long enough to put over the leg of the sweat pants. Not the most attractive look but warm none the less. It would be a great look if you were hiking a mountain or using snowshoes in the wilderness. Yes, ice fishing was pretty much up there too, Maggie thought. She then fiddled with her hair for a few minutes and got it the way she wanted.

Next, she decided to do a small load of laundry. She put in her clothes and the towels that had accumulated. She even noticed a few things of Jack's as well. While they were washing, she carried on cleaning the kitchen. She had a few more dishes to put away and a little sweep around the floor couldn't hurt. Jack was a very tidy man and had a place for everything.

The back door opened giving the cabin an arctic-air type feel.

"Well Maggie, you look great. Are you ready to go ice fishing?" said Jack with enthusiasm.

"Yes, I'm ready," said Maggie as she put on her boots.

Jack helped Maggie with her coat and hat. Maggie wrapped her scarf around her neck and put on her mitts. Jack held onto Maggie's hand as they left the cabin and guided her down to the river's edge.

"This looks very professional, Jack," Maggie said very impressed at the structure of the ice hut.

"It was an amazing buy considering it's insulated, which I didn't know until I put it up today. I guess if I had read the box sooner, I would have known. Before we set foot onto the frozen river there are a couple of things we need to do."

Jack reached down on the bank to grab a rope. One end with a latch was secured around a tree and the other end he wrapped around Maggie's waist and snapped the latch onto the rope. "This is so you don't get lost," he chuckled.

Then Jack reached into a duffle bag and took out a pair of ice picks that were attached to rope at either end. Then he placed them around Maggie's neck. There was a rope with a latch for him as well as a pair of ice picks. Jack was protecting himself and Maggie in case one or both fell in. The ice hut wasn't too far from shore but he wanted to make sure they would be okay. If the ice broke and they fell in the rope would save them from going in too far beneath the water and using the ice picks to grab onto the ice they could pull themselves up onto solid ice, then pulling on the rope they would be able to get to the bank safely. Jack took Maggie's hand and guided her to the hut and unzipped the door.

"Let's go inside, Maggie and don't let go of my hand until you're sitting down," Jack said not wanting her to slip and fall, plus she did seem to be a little accident-prone.

"Okay, Jack," said Maggie as he guided her to a folding chair.

Maggie was glad that Jack made sure everything was safe. In the corner of the hut, she noticed a floatable cushion. Jack said it was used to keep a person afloat if they fell in. Jack had thought of everything and was big on safety. He had to be, she thought, being a state park ranger he had to lead by good example. The hut was warm and sheltered them perfectly. The hole in the ice was just the right size to put their two lines in.

"What kind of bait are we using, Jack?"

"I thought we would try minnows. I saw Kim and Dale when I went to buy some. They wanted me to let you know they said hi and Kim said to tell you to enjoy yourself."

"That's nice of them, and I intend to do just that."

Jack put bait on the lines. Maggie dropped hers down first and stopped it before hitting the bottom. Jack dropped his to the bottom and then reeled it up just off the bottom of the river. Now they waited.

"Do you think we will catch anything, Jack?"

"It's hard to say, you would think they would be hungry because of the cold. But they actually slow down because of the cold and eat less. So, if there is one out there that is hungry, he should bite our line."

"Look, Jack," said Maggie as her rod was bending slightly up and down.

Maggie reeled in her line and caught a nice-sized, largemouth bass. Jack was impressed and happy that she caught one. He put another minnow on her hook and Maggie put down her line. Jack had mentioned the rods were twenty-seven inches long. They were a perfect size to use; she couldn't imagine using a full-size rod, sitting in an ice hut. Maggie was really enjoying herself and so was Jack. They talked about so many things and realized they had more in common than they thought. Jack saw his rod move and started to reel it in. He caught a largemouth too, slightly smaller than Maggie's.

"What do you say we go in and cook these up for lunch?"

"Sounds good to me," said Maggie, as she reeled in her line.

Ready to go Jack unzipped the doorway and helped Maggie out of the ice hut holding on to her hand while carrying the fish on a stringer in his other hand. Placing the fish on the ice Jack zipped up the doorway. Once they got to the river's edge and over the bank Jack unlatched the rope around him and Maggie. Then he took the ice picks from around their necks and put them in the duffle bag. Jack again took Maggie's hand while making their way to the cabin. Reaching the cabin, she asked if he had to put the hut away. He said yes, and that he could do it after lunch. He wanted to fillet the fish so they could eat. Maggie said she could do it while he went and put the ice hut away. Then she could make lunch.

"I forgot you knew how to fillet a fish," said Jack. "This will work out perfect, Maggie. I shouldn't be long."

"Do you have any preference of how you want the fish cooked, Jack?"

"No, surprise me, however you cook it will be okay with me."

Jack went to take down the ice hut. The weather changes so quickly at the park that you really didn't want to leave things on a river that was frozen or not. It would be a great home for the wildlife too once they figured how to get into it. Jack could hear snowmobiles in the distance and wondered if one of them was Dale with his brand-new snowmobile. It was another good buy for sure at the auction. Maybe Maggie would like to go one day as well. Jack was also thinking if it wasn't for Mrs. Murphy running into him at Town Hardware all of this wouldn't have been possible. He wouldn't have seen Maggie; he wouldn't have known Stew wasn't a boyfriend and he wouldn't have been at the auction. He couldn't be happier, having Maggie here with him and having her in his life.

Back at the cabin, Jack put everything away in the shed. As he looked at the wood pile, he thought he better split a few more pieces for the fireplace. He took off his jacket and started splitting the wood. Maggie could hear the axe hitting the wood and came out to see. She loved this whole environment and could stay here forever. Now she knew what Kim was talking about. Enjoy each other's company whenever you can. It's days like this that are very special. Jack stopped to brush the hair out of his eyes. He noticed Maggie watching him.

"Ready to eat?" she asked.

"Yes, I just worked up an appetite. I'll be right in, Maggie."

Maggie went in to put the food on the table and Jack carried in an armful of wood and put it in the metal box. He went outside to get one more load.

"It certainly smells good, Maggie."

Jack washed up and sat down at the dining room table. Maggie had pan broiled the fish with garlic butter, salt and pepper. To go with the fish, she made fresh hash browns and coleslaw. Jack couldn't wait to dig in. He really did work up an appetite plus Maggie cooking a delicious meal didn't hurt either. Maggie poured two cups of coffee then she put two extra pieces of fish on a separate plate incase Jack wanted more. His eyes lit up but his eyes may have been bigger than his stomach.

The calling sound of a Bald Eagle ringtone caught Jack's attention and he reached into his back pocket to get his cell phone. The Bald Eagle was his favourite bird. When he was a boy and went camping with his parents, there was a Bald Eagle that called every morning, sitting on the same tree branch above his tent. Jack thought it was talking to him and would respond to the bird. He called it Valour, because of its strength and courage. He thought it was the most beautiful bird he had ever seen, with its white head and brown sculpted body giving it a majestic appearance. Valour's wingspan was very wide and each feather on its body was meticulously placed. Eventually the bird knew Jack's life story because it showed up every morning for weeks. When it was packing day for the family to leave the park, the bird flew away and Jack wondered if he would ever see it again. Sure enough, when they returned to the same campsite, weeks later, the Bald Eagle was there to greet Jack. This happened throughout the summer months, for two summers, until one day Valour never showed up. Jack was very sad, but his dad told him that the eagle had been there for Jack, when he needed him and now it was time for Valour to continue on his journey that was set out for him. Jack learned at an early age that you make the most of each day and those you encounter along the way.

"Hi, Mom, everything okay?"

"Yes son, I thought you would like to come for supper tonight."

"I have Maggie with me, Mom."

"How nice, invite her too, Jack."

"Maggie, my mom wants us both to come for supper tonight."

"I'd love to Jack; tell your mom thank you."

"Maggie says thank you Mom, will see you tonight around six, I love you too, bye."

"I hope you don't mind Maggie. She calls me up in the spur of the moment to come over to eat. Sometimes it's lunch and sometimes it's breakfast. I find she calls when she is the loneliest. Today it's supper time."

"I don't mind at all; I'm just going to run and put the clothes into the dryer. They weren't ready when we left. I don't want to wear your sweat pants to see your mother."

Jack smiled and carried on with his lunch. It just slipped down so easily. Maggie had filleted the fish nicely. She was quite a girl and he was lucky to have found her. Maggie rejoined Jack at the table quite happy that she would be able to wear her own clothes when they went for supper at his mom's apartment.

"Would you like to go snowmobiling after we eat, Maggie? We can double if you feel safer."

"Yes, I would like that. I have never been snowmobiling before. I've never had the opportunity and I would love to see all the scenery in the park."

Jack and Maggie finished their lunch and cleaned up the dishes together. The leftover fish was put into the refrigerator for tomorrow. While Jack was cleaning the broiling pan Maggie went to get the laundry from the dryer. She folded all the towels and put them away. She put two in the bathroom and the rest in the hall closet. Her clothes came clean, not a wine stain at all. Thank goodness she thought, now she could wear them to see Jack's mom. She took Jack's clothes and hung them in his closet; the rest went into his drawers.

"Are you ready to go, Maggie?" said Jack, as he put two pieces of wood on the fire.

"Yes, be right there."

Jack had his boots and coat on, ready to go. He grabbed his toque and ski gloves and headed outside. Maggie was right behind him, all bundled up in her ski jacket and boots with her scarf, hat and mitts. They walked over to the shed and inside were two snowmobiles. Jack pushed the snowmobile out of the shed using a dolly and then pushed it to the snow where Maggie was standing. He gave her a helmet to wear and he had one as well.

"Why are we taking this one, Jack instead of the other one?"

"This is a double snowmobile. You can only double-up if the snowmobile is made for two people. I'm going to tap you on the leg when I start the engine and again when we are going to move. This way you won't be surprised. Here Maggie, put this harness on and sit on the back. I want to make sure you have a great time and not fall off, since it's your first experience. Also do up your seat belt."

Maggie sat on the back with the harness on and her seat belt connected. Jack went in front of

Maggie. He took the two front straps of the harness and put them around his waist and connected the two tabs into each other. Now Maggie was connected to him. He also did up his seat belt. Now ready, Jack tapped Maggie on the leg. The snowmobile made a lot of noise. Jack tapped Maggie again and they were off, this was quite different for Maggie. The scenery was breathtaking she thought. The trees were all covered in snow and the river was a blanket of snow. It was definitely a winter wonderland. Maggie was seeing the heart of Soul River and it was the attraction where wildlife came to live and people came to visit. She didn't realize just how vast the river was. This was totally different than being in a boat fishing. Within minutes they had traveled the length of the river, following the trail along the river's edge. Maggie would see the park in a different light now. No wonder Jack loves being a park ranger. The excitement of nature's playground was endless. But with this beauty came a responsibility and knowledge of respecting what nature had put fourth because without it there could be misfortune waiting for you. Jack stopped at what seemed like a hilltop. He pointed ahead where two foxes were playing in the snow, unaware that they were being watched, they were having too much fun playing. Jack unbuckled the harness and seat belt then he took off his helmet. He helped Maggie with hers then helped her up from the snowmobile and put his arms around her. Jack gave her a passionate kiss, then hung onto her not wanting to let go.

"I feel like I'm on top of the world, Maggie. This is my favorite place to be in the park. I come here to look over what I am paid to do. But it's more than that. It's where I feel at one with this land and one within myself. But the last time I came I questioned, what was the sense of having all this without someone to share it with? Then I found you Maggie, literally sitting on my doorstep. I knew it the first time we met, when you hooked me, and the day I helped you out of the river. The evening, we spent talking and having coffee and the time I saw you outside the hardware store in another man's arms. I'm falling in love with you Maggie Sinclaire. I know it's soon to be saying all this, but I can't deny how I feel. I hope that maybe you feel the same way too or at least a little."

The look in Jack's eyes was captivating and his words were endearing, and heartfelt. Maggie could see he needed to get it off his chest and for him to bring her to his special place meant everything to her.

"I feel the same way, Jack; I'm falling in love with you too. I know we haven't known each other very long, but I do believe that people are sent our way for a reason. I can't deny either, how I feel, Jack Kincaid. You feel like home to me and I don't want that feeling to ever go away."

Jack was so happy that Maggie felt the same way. Maggie and Jack kissed and held each other tight. They stood there looking at the snow-covered river that had stopped in time. For at that moment, they too were in their own little world.

CHAPTER 25

Maggie took her coffee to the living room and set it on the table beside the sofa, as she waited for her mom to answer the phone.

"Hi, Mom, how are you?" she said, as Jasper came and sat down next to her feet.

"Oh, that's great, glad to hear that. Yes . . . yes, I had a great time. Yes . . . you would like him, Mom. Jack is a wonderful man. I'm lucky to have met him," Maggie said, taking a sip of her coffee. "Yesterday he took me to meet his mother. Her name is Hannah. She is very much like Jack, warm and loving," she said smiling, as she took another sip of her coffee. "Oh yeah, I remember Mom. Hmm . . . I don't know . . . I would have to ask Jack. Okay, I will let you know. Uh-huh . . . yes, since the drive-thru opened . . . we have sold a lot of coffee. Oh, yes, for sure. Grandmother would be so proud. How is your business doing? Mm-hmm, mm-hmm... Yes, me too. I know . . . I can't believe we've been talking that long," said Maggie as she got up to look out the window. "Yes, later today. I wish you could come and visit. All right, yes . . . uh-huh . . . Love you too, bye Mom."

Maggie went to the kitchen to pour herself a second cup of coffee and put kibble in Jasper's dish. She was so happy that she talked to her mother and was able to tell her about Jack.

"Well, Jasper, we have a big day today. Do you miss Tilly, I bet you do? Here, come eat your breakfast. Good boy," she said as she patted Jasper's head.

Maggie took her coffee into the bathroom and put it on the vanity as usual. Into the shower she went. Today she had to make sure she went to work. It was cookie-making day for Maggie. She needed to make boxes of cookies for the Carleton Falls Town Square Christmas tree. After the bakery closes Charlie and Jack are going to make cookies with Maggie. She stepped out of the shower and put a pair of jeans on and a t-shirt. This pretty Christmas sweater is coming with me she decided and put it in a bag to take with her. She towel-dried her hair and fixed her curls. She felt in a Christmassy mood. It was the cookies and thinking about the tree lighting at the town square. Only a few days left to get things ready for those last-minute shoppers. The bakery should be non-stop today, Maggie thought. She grabbed her boots and coat. Out the door she went with Jasper at her side. Jack had taken the snow off her car when he dropped her off last night. Just thinking of him made her happy.

Maggie dropped Jasper off at Flora's house. She was right about the bakery being busy. It had just opened and it seems everyone had the same idea. Get there early before it gets busy. Maggie went through the back door to the back room to change. She changed her jeans and put on the Christmas sweater she brought with her.

"Good morning, Julie, good morning, Noah," said Maggie.

"Good morning, Maggie," said Julie with a smile on her face. "You're in a happy mood so early in the morning."

"Good morning to you too, Maggie," said Noah.

"It's because it's cookie day and I love cookie day. Noah did you get moved okay?" Maggie said changing the subject.

"Yes, I did, Maggie. My friends made sure of that. I really like my place, the town and my job," said Noah as he put some pies into the oven.

"I'm glad," said Maggie.

Julie looked over at Maggie giving her head a shake. She knew what Maggie was doing. She didn't want her to ask about Jack. Maggie went out front to see the girls and to make sure everything was good. Ella had decorated the bakery for Christmas. Maggie knew it was Ella because she had a certain way of putting things together and she loved Christmas lights. Liz showed Maggie that there was only one of Alice's Coffee left on the shelf. She also let Maggie know that she has had great feedback about the coffee. This made Maggie happy and she would have to package more today. You can't sell what you don't have. Through the window Maggie saw Mr. Parker Alexander picking up his cheesecake orders from the delivery area. Noah was talking to him and shaking his hand. Maggie went back to speak to Mr. Alexander as well. She needed to thank him in person for sending Noah her way. He said he needed to know that she had another baker on the premises besides Julie and herself because he was going to up his order and he wanted to make sure they could handle it. Maggie smiled, gave him a hug and wished him a Merry Christmas.

Maggie brought all the ingredients for Alice's Coffee to the back table and mixed them. She got the boxes and filled them up then placed them on the shelf out front. The plum pudding pies were almost sold out. She went to see if there were more in the walk-in. She had five in her hands, and another eight, left in the walk-in. That would probably take them to lunchtime.

Because her staff were great employees, she wanted to order a few pizzas from Phil's Pizza Palace and have them delivered.

"Hi, Phil, it's Maggie, how are you?"

"I'm good, Maggie, what can I get for you?"

"I would like to order four large pizzas with the works."

"Pick up or delivery."

"It will have to be delivery Phil, I'm just too busy to come and visit you."

"I know the feeling, I definitely understand," said Phil as the other phone started ringing. "Bye, Maggie."

Maggie went out front to tell the girls and to let them know once delivered they could come back any time to have a slice. It was an eat-as-you-go day, Maggie told them. Mrs. Abigail was at the counter getting some cream puffs for her card playing group.

"Hello, Mrs. Abigail, how are you?" said Maggie.

"I'm good, keeping busy. I just love your cream puffs Maggie and so do the ladies. You know I tried making some cream puffs one day. I didn't realize that they were so hard to make. Mine turned a golden brown but didn't rise. I thought if I filled them with whipped cream they would expand. Nope, they were like an old inner tube, flat and tough," laughed Mrs. Abigail making her whole face light up.

Her laughter was contagious as even some of Maggie's other customers couldn't help but laugh and smile.

"One day we will get together and I will show you how to make them, Mrs. Abigail. They're really not that hard to make."

"Thank you dear, I would like that. Well, you have yourself a nice day, Merry Christmas."

"You too Mrs. Abigail, Merry Christmas."

Maggie saw two more familiar faces sitting in the corner of the room. She was happy to see them and had to go and talk to them.

"Merry Christmas, Mr. and Mrs. Litmann, it's so nice to see you."

"And a Merry Christmas to you too, Maggie. Your bakery is doing a wonderful business and the drive-thru, that was brilliance," said Mr. Litmann.

"I wish I could take the credit but it was Mrs. Murphy. She envisioned it," said Maggie as she looked over at Mrs. Litmann. "What do you both do now to fill your days since you don't have the business?"

"We are pretty much retired, since we sold the property to you. We'll be spending Christmas with our children and after that we will be going to Florida until spring."

"I'm so happy for you; it was nice seeing you both."

"And you, Maggie."

Maggie went to the back to see if the pizzas had been delivered. She was just about to ask Julie when there was a knock at the door. There were four hot delicious-smelling pizzas. Maggie paid the deliveryman along with giving him a tip and wished him a Merry Christmas as well.

"Julie and Noah, help yourselves to pizza whenever you want one, I will let the girls know out front."

Maggie told the girls about the pizza. She wanted to get started on the boxed cookies for the tree. One of the mixers wasn't being used, so Maggie put in the ingredients and turned it on. She took a slice of pizza while she was waiting. Mmm . . . she thought as she took the first bite, heavenly. It didn't take her long to finish it as she hadn't eaten all day. After washing her hands, she sprinkled some flour on the table. Then she took the dough from the mixer and put it on the table. She made a double batch, took a portion of the dough and rolled it out for the first tray of cookies. She used one cookie cutter for each tray. That way the cookies would stack better in each box. She would make Christmas trees, stars, snowmen, bells, candy canes, Santas, and stockings. Once she got started, it didn't take long. She had to remember to put a hole into the dough of each cookie before it was cooked. This way you would be able to hang them on the tree.

Julie and Noah had taken a short break then started making pies for the freezer.

"Maggie, before I forget to tell you, Jimmy delivered the apples from Mr. Mason. You were up front when he came."

"Thanks, Julie, I would have forgotten to ask you."

Maggie had finished boxing all the cookies she had made. The electric dough sheeter certainly came in handy rolling the dough out. It took most of the afternoon but it would have taken much longer with a rolling pin. There was one box of pizza left. She thought she would leave it out incase Charlie or Jack would like some. Maggie let everyone go home early and said she would take care of the last hour alone. As long as she could keep up with the drive-thru it should be okay. There was a couple at a table eating scones and having a coffee. They had one of Maggie's cake boxes on the table too. They told Maggie they came from Wesbridge. They had seen the article in the Hainesley newspaper and finally came to see what everyone was talking about. They told Maggie they loved the bakery and the coffee was outstanding. It was well worth the drive and they would definitely come back. Maggie thanked them and went back to the drive-thru.

"One black coffee please and one coffee anyway you want it," said a deep rugged voice.

"Jack, you're early and I'm so glad. Come on in and we'll have one together. It's almost time to close anyway."

The couple at the table had left and it was ten to five. Jack entered the bakery and couldn't wait to give Maggie a hug and a kiss. She poured two cups of coffee and gave Jack one, then she handed him a hairnet.

"No way," he laughed.

"Yes, why do you think I wear one?"

"To keep your hair nice."

"No, all employees wear them to make sure no hair gets in the food. Here I will help you, Jack."

"Okay, if I must," said Jack. "I just came to make cookies."

"Stop being a baby, it's painless, I promise," said Maggie, helping Jack put it on. "You look so handsome."

"And you look beautiful in your Christmas sweater," said Jack as he gave Maggie another kiss.

She reached under the sink to get a cloth and a spray bottle of disinfectant. She sprayed the tables out front and wiped them down. She felt Jack's eyes on her the whole time. She then cleaned the counter and the drive-thru area.

"What did you do today, Jack?"

"Oh, pretty much the usual. I took the snowmobile out to check the park and made sure everything was in order. People came to skate again today and there were three guys ice fishing."

"It sounds like you had a busy day too. I missed you and it was hard going to work today. I wanted to be at the park too. But you're here now."

"I missed you too, Maggie." Jack said as he gave her another kiss.

"Jack, I wonder where Charlie is. It's not like him to be late. Well, he knows to come in the back door. So, I'm going to lock up and turn the lights off."

Maggie and Jack carried their coffees to the back.

"Charlie," called Maggie, "why didn't you let us know you were here?"

"I didn't want to interrupt you two. If I had, you might have gotten one less kiss or two, so you should be thanking me."

"Oh Charlie, you're so funny. Don't ever stop being you," said Maggie as she looked at Jack with a smile. "Would you like a coffee, Charlie?"

"No, thank you, maybe later."

"I see you have a hairnet on Charlie," said Jack.

"Yes, I know the rules, clean apron too, here's yours. These are the perks of making cookies."

Maggie went to get the ingredients while Jack and Charlie got reacquainted. Maggie started up two mixers. Maggie had them wash their hands while they were waiting for her. She sprinkled flour over the table, then she had them take out the dough from the mixers and put it on the floured table. She put Charlie on her one side and Jack on the other. This way they could watch her to see what to do. Maggie gave them each some dough and asked them to roll it out to about a quarter inch thick. This was great she thought as she watched them maneuver their rolling pin. They were very meticulous and one would even think there was a competition going on to see who rolled out the dough better. Maggie just smiled to herself and placed some cookie cutters in front of them. Jack and Charlie were asked to pick one cookie cutter each. Jack picked the tree, he said it reminded him of the park and Charlie picked the snowman, it reminded him of the ones he used to make with his sister when they were kids. They watched Maggie as she used her candy cane cutter, then they started on their dough. While they were cutting their dough Maggie went to get three cookie trays and placed one in front of each of them. Maggie took her cut cookies and placed them on her pan. Watching Maggie, Jack and Charlie did the same.

"That wasn't too bad," said Jack, never having made cookies before.

"Aw . . . you're not done yet," said Charlie, having been through the cookie process before.

Maggie chuckled as the two went back and forth as Charlie tried to tell Jack what was coming next.

"Your right, Charlie," Maggie said, "but you forgot what we do with the leftover dough scraps on the table after we cut out the cookies."

"I know," said Jack, "we put them in the scrap pile."

They all laughed and Maggie showed them that they take the scraps, put them into a ball and roll it out again. Then they cut more cookies and placed them on the tray. Once the cookie tray was full into the oven they went.

"Where's Jasper tonight, Maggie?" asked Charlie.

"Flora said she would watch him. I still can't believe how Jasper calms Tilly down. Jasper is a pretty special dog. He seems to sense the emotions of people and other animals."

"He is a great dog, Maggie," said Jack playing with a piece of dough.

Maggie suggested taking a break and having some pizza. The boy's agreed and she slipped a few slices into the oven. She also put a bowl over each ball of dough sitting on the table so it wouldn't dry out while they were eating. Maggie poured everyone a coffee as they talked about the experience so far. The number one question was; when could they eat one? Maggie let them know after all the cookies were iced and decorated, they could have one of their creations. Maggie realized how Jack and Charlie were alike. One thing for sure they liked to tease her and make her laugh. Charlie took his coffee and went outside to get some fresh air.

Jack made his move now that he and Maggie were alone. He placed his arms around her and gave her a passionate kiss. She returned the kiss with just as much passion. They were really in love and from the looks of it, Charlie knew when it was time for him to let them have some alone time. After all he was young once and he wanted Maggie to have someone in her life. He really thought Jack was a great guy for Maggie. So much in fact Jack reminded Charlie of Walter, Maggie's dad.

Now that everyone had a break, they were back at making cookies. Jack's next pick was a star, because of the stars at night when he goes camping. Charlie's next pick was a stocking. His mother use to put his and his sister's Christmas stocking at the end of their beds because they didn't have a fireplace to hang them. This way Santa would fill them and they could open them when they woke up. He laughed as he told the story. As he and his sister got older, they realized it just kept them busy so mom and dad could sleep in, Christmas morning. Maggie and Jack laughed as they remembered their own childhood Christmas stories.

Two batches were out of the oven and cooling off. The third batch was ready to be baked. Charlie and Jack cleaned the large commercial mixers for Maggie. Now the icing for the cookies could be made. Maggie told the boys what ingredients were needed and handed them a mixing bowl each and a spatula to mix with. Once it was mixed Charlie spooned the white icing into a piping bag. Jack needed to add green food colouring into his mixture. He then added his green icing into a piping bag. Each of them took their cooled cookie tray and put it in front of them. They watched Maggie go first. She showed them to squeeze the bag slowly and guide the piping tip along the edge of the cookie then fill in the middle. Maggie was very quick at it and finished before the boys. She made the rest of the icing colours needed to finish the cookies, red, black and yellow then put them in separate piping bags.

"How are we doing?" Maggie said, interrupting Jack and Charlie talking about Jack's ice fishing hut.

"All done," said Charlie, waiting for the next step.

"Here, Charlie, a piping bag of black and one red for you. I'll do one to show you and then you do the rest."

Jack was watching as well. Maggie made the snowman's hat black. She then put three black buttons on the body. The face came next as she put two black eyes on and placed a little orange candy decoration dipped in a little icing for the nose. She took the red piping bag and made a smiling mouth. Next, she added a red scarf around the snowman's neck and down his chest. The red was also used to make stripes on Charlie's candy canes. Now it was Jack's turn. Maggie took the yellow piping bag and made garland from side to side all the way down the tree. Next, she took little round-coloured decorations and put them on the garland and pressed a bit so they would stick. The star cookies were done with the yellow icing and white sprinkles were added for decoration.

Four hours had passed and they were done. The cookies looked great and worthy to sell in the bakery. Charlie and Jack looked at Maggie. With an affirmative shake of Maggie's head, the guys took a bite of one of their cookies. "Mmm . . ." they both said as they devoured them.

"These are really good, Maggie," said Jack wanting another one.

"Have a couple more if you want. I'm going to pack some for you to take home anyway, you both deserve it. We will have to make this a Christmas tradition from now on."

Jack and Charlie agreed and indulged in a couple more cookies. This time Maggie made coffee to go with them. Waiting for the coffee Maggie boxed an assortment of cookies for Jack and Charlie to take home. The rest she put into containers and stacked them in the walk-in for the showcase tomorrow and any orders that Julie had. The guys really did a great job and they got along so well Maggie thought. Now they were talking about the Carleton Falls Mercantile Charlie had before he retired. Jack was so interested how Charlie had started a pharmacy in Carleton Falls and his need to help the people. Charlie had great insight Jack thought and was a good businessman as well.

Maggie took a sip of her coffee and thought how nice it would be if they all spent Christmas Day together. Since her mother had moved to Italy, Maggie never really bothered about Christmas. She never even put up a Christmas tree. She would always ask Charlie over for Christmas dinner, but it wasn't anything fancy. This year she wanted it to be different. She wanted all the trimmings that went along with Christmas. She even wanted Hannah, Jack's mother to be a part of it all. Maybe

Charlie and Hannah would enjoy each other's company.

Charlie left for home and picked up Jasper from Flora's house on the way. The kitchen still needed to be cleaned so Maggie and Jack had taken on that job. Jack was a great help and worked the commercial dishwasher like a pro. While he was doing that Maggie cleaned all the tables and mopped the floor. They were tired and it was getting quite late. Maggie suggested Jack come back to her place and stay the night instead of going back to the park. Jack thought it was a great idea.

CHAPTER 26

"This one is beautiful Jack, let's get this one, it's perfect," said Maggie, so happy how the afternoon was going.

"I have to admit, you picked a good one," said Jack. "Mr. Mason, we'll take this one."

"Good choice, spruce has always been my favourite Christmas tree. How are you two doing?"

"We're good, Mr. Mason," said Maggie as she watched Jack load the tree into the cargo bed of his truck. "Are you going to watch the Christmas tree lighting tonight?"

"I wouldn't miss it and haven't missed one in all these years," said Mr. Mason.

"I have all the boxed cookies ready and there should be a good-sized crowd," said Maggie. "This year Randy Timms is going to have some of the choir there to sing Christmas carols. Last night, Jack and I went to see a Christmas play at the church then afterwards we went to one of the eggnog parties. We'll see you tonight, Mr. Mason. Thank you and have a Merry Christmas," said Maggie as she got into Jack's truck.

"Well, you have one too, Maggie."

"C'mon, Jasper, get in boy," said Jack as he went to give Mr. Mason a hand shake and wish him a Merry Christmas.

"I wonder how your mom's doing with her stuffing?" said Maggie.

"I'm sure she is having a great time making it. She loves to cook," said Jack smiling, thinking how it used to be.

It had snowed again last night and everything was covered in that white blanket that nature provided this time of year. The sun had come out and the snow on the roads had melted. As Jack pulled in Maggie's driveway, they saw the productive time Charlie had spent putting up Christmas lights. The shrubs were all covered with coloured lights. He even had a Santa and a snowman on the front lawn.

"Looks good, Charlie," Jack said as he got out of his truck.

Jasper couldn't wait to see Charlie and squeezed between the two front seats to get out the driver's door. Off he ran and nudged Charlie in the shin as he was adding a string of lights to a small tree.

"Okay, boy, I love you too," said Charlie as he patted Jasper on the head. "Do you need any help bringing the tree inside, Jack?"

"No, I'm good, as long as Maggie can get the door."

Maggie took the parcels from the back seat and opened the front door for Jack.

"Where do you want it, hun?" Jack said, waiting for Maggie to let him know.

"I'm not sure, Jack."

"What about over there, in this corner. We can move this chair over here."

"Yes, Hannah, that's a great spot; we'll be able to see it from every direction."

"The stuffing smells great, Mom," said Jack. "I can't wait until tomorrow."

Hannah always made her stuffing the day or evening before. It was one less thing to do Christmas day and the stuffing was always tastier because the flavours were enhanced by it sitting overnight. Maggie and Charlie also commented on the wonderful smell of stuffing throughout the house. Maggie was also happy that the bakery was only open until noon. It gave her and Jack time to do last minute shopping and get a tree.

Jack put the tree in the corner where the girls wanted it. All they had to do was decorate it. With the decorations Hannah had and the ones Maggie had the tree would look great. Charlie and Jack put on the sparkling white lights first then each ornament was placed in just the right spot; Maggie and Hannah saw to that. Once they were done, they all stood back to see the result. The tree looked beautiful but there was something missing and they all knew what it was. They didn't have anything for the top of the tree. They all looked a little dismayed and were trying to figure out what they could use. Hannah asked Maggie if she had any white construction paper. The guys were wondering why Hannah would want some paper and so was Maggie. Maggie said she had some and went to get it. Maggie came back and gave Hannah the paper.

They all watched Hannah as she folded and then folded the paper again. They all sat mystified as she kept folding the paper. When she finished, she had made the most beautiful paper angel Maggie had ever seen and Charlie was just as amazed. Jack had forgotten about that eventful night many years ago. One Christmas when he was a young boy, he accidentally broke the angel for their tree. Hannah being the mother she was didn't want Jack to be upset and made him an origami angel. He went over and gave Hannah a big hug and a kiss on the cheek. Maggie thanked Hannah and gave her a hug too and asked Jack if he would put it on top of the tree. Once again, they all stood back, finally the tree was complete. They were all having a wonderful afternoon. The tree looked beautiful Maggie thought. Then she looked at how happy Jack was having his mother here and she had never seen Charlie smile so much.

Besides the stuffing, Hannah had made her famous lasagna for supper and it had been cooking in the oven while they decorated the tree. They all sat down to eat in the dining room and the conversation started about the tree lighting ceremony. Maggie got up to get the rolls left on the kitchen counter. Jack made an excuse to get the butter that was already on the table. Charlie and Hannah knew what they were up to and just smiled at each other. Hannah was so happy spending Christmas with Jack, Maggie and Charlie. This was what she needed and so did Charlie. It was surprising to both of them just how much they had in common. Maggie new they would hit it off right away.

"Jack, what are you looking for?" said Maggie with the roll basket in her hand.

"I'm looking for you, Miss Sinclaire."

Maggie put down the rolls and put her arms on Jack's shoulders. He wrapped his arms around her and gave her a kiss.

"This is the best Christmas I have had in years," said Jack. "I'm finally with the people I should be with and the people I love the most. Even Charlie has become family."

"I know exactly what you mean, Jack, I feel the same way."

After one last kiss they went back to join Hannah and Charlie who were so absorbed in their own conversation that they didn't even know Maggie and Jack were back sitting at the table.

"Delicious meal, Hannah," said Charlie as he helped clear the table. "I don't remember the last time I had lasagna. I can only imagine what the turkey is going to taste like. I can still smell the stuffing."

Hannah smiled and was happy to feel useful again. She had always hoped that Jack would find someone and settle down. It finally happened and Hannah thought the world of Maggie. This Christmas wasn't only special for Jack and Maggie, it was very special to Hannah and Charlie. Both had been alone far too long and realized that a little companionship would be nice.

"Here, Mom," Jack said as he cleared the last bowl from the table. "Now you and Charlie just relax, Maggie and I will take care of the dishes."

"Hannah, why don't we take Jasper out front for a run and look at the Christmas lights. The timer should have turned them on by now," said Charlie.

"I'd like that, Charlie," she said as she headed to the front closet to get her boots and coat.

Charlie helped Hannah with her coat and then slipped on his own. He had a little trouble with his boots and Hannah saw a shoe horn hanging on the wall inside the closet. It was a long one so Charlie didn't have to bend down. Jasper was eager to get outside after he heard his name called. The front light display that Charlie had arranged looked wonderful.

"You did a beautiful job, Charlie," Hannah said. "The coloured lights are stunning and this is the only house on the street with coloured lights. They really stand out."

As Charlie stepped back, he said the last time he saw lights on this house at Christmas was when Maggie's dad Walter was alive. Jack has brought life back into this house he told Hannah. He also told her that she was an added bonus to the Maggie and Jack relationship. Hannah smiled and told Charlie she enjoyed his company too. They both stood side by side looking at the lights and watching Jasper running around in the snow wearing off energy. At times he would stop and roll in it, then get up and shake the snow off. When he came and sat at

Charlie's side, Charlie knew it was time to take him in.

"How do the lights look?" asked Jack, as Hannah and Charlie came through the front door with Jasper.

"They're beautiful," said Hannah, "Charlie couldn't have done a better job. Is Maggie still doing dishes?"

"No, the dishes are done. She's just freshening up and said we should be leaving for the tree ceremony."

Charlie said he would drive his car because there would be more room in the back seat, instead of Jack's truck. Maggie's car had her delivery food cooler in her hatchback and she needed a good size trunk for all the boxed cookies. Charlie didn't mind as he would have Hannah in the passenger seat to talk to, while Maggie and Jack rode in the back seat holding hands. Jasper stayed home where he would be warm and cozy. After all the physical activity he had running and playing in the snow he fell right to sleep on his dog bed.

The streets were all lit up with Christmas lights and the people were starting their cars, getting ready to leave for the tree lighting ceremony. As they passed by the houses, they saw some parents waving their kids on to hurry up. They had to stop by the bakery first to pick up the boxed cookies. The wish cookies were Maggie's favourite thing to do and it meant so much to her. It was a tradition her grandmother did with her at Christmas time. Alice would make a special cookie for Maggie and on Christmas Eve she gave it to Maggie and had her make a wish, then placed it on the Christmas tree. This wasn't just any wish. Maggie had to think long and hard if she wanted to make a wish for her or someone else. Alice told Maggie that in a year people had so many things happen to them, a lot of exciting things and some not so nice things. At the end of that year one wish could give them hope again for themselves, for people they love or just someone they saw that they thought could benefit from that wish. Maggie wanted to pass on Alice's tradition but in a much bigger way. She thought if the whole town made wishes on the same night just think how the people of Carleton Falls could spread compassion, love and kindness for one another in only one wish times hundreds.

Charlie parked around back and unlocked the trunk of his car. Maggie and Jack went in to get the cookies. It was snowing now, gently falling as Maggie looked up to the sky to see the stars shining through the falling snowflakes. She smiled at Jack as they loaded the cookies. After three trips they were ready to go. The town looked beautiful for Christmas as each business had out did themselves in decorating. Charlie pulled into the town square so Maggie and Jack could unload the cookies. Hannah also got out of the car while Charlie went to park at the back of the property.

People had already started entering the town square. Maggie started handing out her cookies. Each cookie came with a string so the person could put it through the hole in the cookie and tie it together. Most of the people knew about the cookie and the wish they were to make. But some new residents were pleasantly surprised that someone would do such a nice thing, something special that brought the people together.

The tree was starting to fill up nicely and Ray Fletcher from city hall had a set of moveable stairs beside the tree so the cookies could be put even higher up in the tree this year. Everyone took their time while some sipped on hot chocolate. Mrs. Murphy had asked Ray if they could serve hot chocolate to the public. He thought it was a great idea and made it happen.

Randy Timms and the choir were standing behind the tree on a platform singing Christmas carols. Some people were singing along and others were chatting away, seeing people they hadn't seen in a while. Charlie and Hannah were mingling as well and Jack was on the stairs making sure no one slipped. They also had a pole that you could hook the cookie onto then reach up and place your cookie on a higher branch of the tree. Maggie saw some people standing in front of the tree thinking about their wish. Others knew what it would be right away and immediately placed their cookie on the Christmas tree. Some parents were explaining to their children about the cookie on the tree and what it meant. Jack looked over at Maggie and saw her having a wonderful time. She was explaining to a little boy about the cookie and how special it really was. Maggie watched as the little boy stood quietly closing his eyes and making a wish then placed his cookie on the tree. Maybe that little boy will someday think back to when a lady gave him a wish cookie and told him how important it was.

Jack went to see Maggie as two city hall employees took the stairs and rolled them into a city truck. It had stopped snowing and there were only four cookies left to be put on the tree.

"The countdown to light up the Carleton Fall's Town Square Christmas tree will begin in two minutes," announced Ray Fletcher.

Maggie went over to Charlie and Hannah and gave them a cookie each. Then she gave one to Jack and kept the other one for herself. They all approached the tree and made their wishes. No one asked the other what their wish was as they all knew it wouldn't come true if they told, and even if it didn't, it didn't matter anyway, because the cookie did its job bringing the people of Carleton Falls together.

"Ten . . . nine . . . eight . . . seven . . . six . . . five . . . four . . . three . . . two . . . one!"

CHAPTER 27

Well, there you have it. It took a while but we got there. Yes, yes, Maggie and Jack finally got together. If ever two people were destined to be together, it was them. Everyone else saw it before they did. I guess you wonder what happened next. Do you really want to know? Oh well, I don't think I will ruin it for you. Maggie and Jack do eventually get married and boy what a wedding it was. Guess who made the wedding cake and desserts for their wedding. Yep, Maggie herself. It was really a Carleton Falls affair since everyone in town knew they were meant for each other; anyone at the Halloween dance could see that, but they had to find out for themselves. Who do you think walked her down the aisle? Yep, it was me, Charlie. Sue had come home for the wedding and we had a lot of laughs. Sue was a different person. Italy was good for her. She was happy, happier than I have seen her in a long time. She got to meet Hannah and they really got along wonderfully. Sue said she could leave for Italy again knowing Hannah was there to help Maggie if she needed her.

Katie was Maggie's matron of honour with both Kim and Julie being a bride's maid. These three girls threw Maggie the biggest wedding shower the town had ever seen at Katie's Bed and Breakfast. It was a money shower. Maggie and Jack had everything they needed house wise but for their honeymoon Maggie wanted to go to Italy. She wanted to see the little town her grandmother, Alice was born in. For the first week Maggie and Jack stayed in a hotel in the town Sue lives in and was born in. A beautiful friendly little town with a picturesque countryside. Maggie could see why Sue didn't want to leave Italy. She had made Italy her home. They loved her shop; Maggie was so impressed at what her mother had accomplished. They had a great time with Sue and Jack was so happy to finally get to know Maggie's mother.

The second week was spent at a hotel in Alice's hometown. Maggie found out so much talking to some of the older residents and they explained a lot; why Alice was the kind of person she was. She didn't have much and worked hard for everything she wanted. They told Maggie that a lot of the time people weren't paid cash for their work. People gave each other items that they needed. If Alice baked a pie for someone who wanted a pie, then they would give her something she wanted like meat or milk, whatever the agreement was. Alice's parents lived in hard times and Alice growing up the same way wanted better for her family, which is why Alice eventually moved her family to Carleton Falls.

Now when it came to the bakery Maggie was still thinking of expanding it. She hasn't yet but if she does, she will call on Mr. Sands to do it. Jack, he is happier than ever working at Carleton Falls State Park and being married to Maggie. You're probably wondering where they live. Well, Jack commutes back and forth and sometimes they both stay at the cabin. With the team Maggie has working at Magpie Bakery she can stay with Jack at the cabin a night or two. It's their getaway place. Maggie wanted Hannah to move in with her and Jack, this way she is closer to them and me. Hannah and I have been spending a lot of time together too. I can't tell you where it's headed, because we like it just the way it is, but you never know.

Oh, and then there is Mrs. Murphy. She is still going strong with her church endeavours and fundraisers. Remember Kent Newsley, he owns Soul River Marina, well anyway Mrs. Murphy and him finally got together and are dating. It was Mrs. Murphy that finally made the first move. She overheard Jenny Smith talking to Betty Derwood at the diner that Kent was interested in Ellen but he was too shy to ask her out. It seemed it was all over town and everyone knew except Mrs. Murphy. So, Mrs. Murphy asked him out on a date and they have been together ever since.

As for Jenny Smith, well, she still sings in the choir and I can tell you her singing voice hasn't gotten any better. I heard her one day practicing in the church auditorium and her voice was as off tune as it gets. She's a great lady and as long as her voice isn't breaking any windows, no one seems to care. You're probably wondering why I was at church. Well, Hannah and I go every Sunday. She is a great influence for sure. I've lost ten pounds just knowing her.

Then . . . let me see, Stew and Emma. Everyone remembers Stew; he was the guy Jack was jealous of. Well, Stew and Emma had a beautiful wedding too. They were married New Years Eve. It was a very big affair and at least half the town was invited. I'm exaggerating, it was less than half the town, but you know what I mean. Maggie had a lot to do that day making delicious desserts and making their beautiful wedding cake. Everything had to be fresh and delivered on time. They are expecting now and will have a little one in the fall.

Katie and Tony's little girl Kat is walking and getting into everything. Katie had ordered a large slab cake from Maggie for a conference. It was beautifully decorated and she put it on the conference table for the people coming. Of course, Kat was with Katie and Katie took her eyes off of Kat, for what seemed only seconds. During that time, Kat got up on a chair and fell into the cake. Katie was beside herself with people coming any minute and Kat, well, she got her first taste of sugar and she loved it. Maggie became Kat's godmother and Jack her godfather. They don't all get together as much as they would like but Maggie still does Katie's luncheons three times a year showing groups of people how to make baked goods from scratch. Other ladies also have demonstrating workshops at Katie's Bed and Breakfast too, demonstrating their talents. Like Julie, the bunch of asparagus girl; she has been demonstrating her sewing skills.

Kim and Dale still run the store at Carleton Falls State Park. Dale was Jack's best man. Dale and Jack do a lot of snowmobiling together. The snowmobile he bought at the auction was a very good one and just like Jack he got a bargain at the price he paid. He never regretted buying it. Kim sees a lot more of Maggie, since her and Jack got married and that's because of her and Jack staying at the cabin at the State Park. Kim has been quite happy the last little while. Don't tell anyone, but Kim and Dale are going to have a baby. The word isn't out there yet, so keep it to yourself.

As for Noah, the guy who should be on a magazine cover, he is dating Liz. They make a real nice couple. The way they look at each other is the same way Maggie and Jack look at each other. But like everyone else they will have to find out for themselves.

Ella and Mark are engaged. If it wasn't for Maggie and her drive-thru Mark would never have met Ella. He is still working for Mr. Sands and has become lead foreman. With the help of Sands 'n Sons Construction Mark is going to have a house built for him and Ella. The plans are already in the works.

Hmm . . . oh yeah, Mr. and Mrs. Litmann, they came back from Florida for the birth of their grandson. He was their first grandson and they were so proud. He was unexpected as they thought their daughter was having another girl. They already have five granddaughters and never thought they would ever have a grandson. Needless to say, they were very happy. So happy in fact they might not go back to Florida.

Then, there are Maggie's Jasper Cookies. Sherry from Pet Start can't seem to keep them on the shelf. She has them in all her stores which, is keeping Maggie very busy. Maggie has since tried her new dog treat called Ca-nine Veggie Bites at Pet Start. They have nine nutritional ingredients in them and they're selling quite well too. What a girl, she is. As for Alice's Coffee, it sold so well that Maggie is getting orders from retail stores in Hainesley.

Now let's see, Jasper has a larger family for sure. He has so many people watching him, he is always kept busy. Jasper likes to follow Hannah around the same as he does with Maggie. He's with Jack more often and loves the outdoors as much as Jack does. The people that come to visit expect to see him with Jack. Jasper has become an important part of Carleton Falls State Park, so much so, that in the brochure the park gives out there is a picture of Jack and Jasper.

Flora still sees Jasper when Maggie brings him to work. Tilly, doesn't have anxiety problems anymore. She is the calmest, the sweetest and the most loveable dog you would ever want to meet. Flora is so grateful for Tilly finding Jasper that day and the flight of the grasshopper. That day changed both their lives. Flora entered Tilly in a dog show just to see how she would react and present herself. She won second prize in her division. Flora couldn't believe it and was so proud of Tilly.

Now you see there were so many things that happened since that Christmas Eve. Oh . . . I forgot to tell you about Hannah's stuffing on Christmas Day. It was so delicious and the best I ever tasted. The turkey she cooked was amazing, so moist and tender. I had seconds and I even had room for Maggie's plum pudding pie. Christmas day was when Jack asked Maggie to marry him. It was only a matter of time and they both knew it. Their engagement wasn't long either. They both just wanted to start their lives together.

Speaking of Christmas day, Jane from Lockmore Jewellers and her family got a wonderful surprise. Her father and my good friend Edward, had regained awareness and is showing signs of improvement from his brain injury. His family thought it was a Christmas miracle. I couldn't be happier for them.

So that's about it. Everyone else is doing well. As for the tree lighting, it was a great success, especially Maggie and her wish cookies. I don't know if everyone got their wish but I do know that Carleton Falls is thriving and everyone seems happy. As for me, I got my wish and more.

About the Author

Sandra Muzyka has a son and a daughter and six grandchildren. She lives in Ontario, Canada with her husband, and their two cats. She has been writing poems and drawing for many, many years as well as writing children's books. She has put her dreams on paper for all to see.